DEADLY IN NEW YORK

DEADLY IN NEW YORK

RANDY WAYNE
WHITE
WRITING AS CARL RAMM

OPEN ROAD
INTEGRATED MEDIA
NEW YORK

Cover design by Andy Ross

ISBN: 978-1-5040-3517-0

This edition published in 2016 by Open Road Integrated Media, Inc.
180 Maiden Lane
New York, NY 10038
www.openroadmedia.com

DEADLY IN NEW YORK

ONE

Little Cayman Island, British West Indies

The assassin who had followed James Hawker from New York to Miami, from Miami to this tiny Caribbean island south of Cuba, stood outside the row of seaside cabanas in the darkness.

He pulled back his cotton worsted leisure jacket and drew the .38 Colt Detective from its holster. The two-inch barrel had been machined for a sound arrester. The silencer was cool in his hands as he screwed it into place.

He waited a full minute before he moved again.

A fresh wind drifted off the reef, and the tropic moon was a gaseous orange above the line of coconut palms.

The assassin, whose name was Renard, moved closer to the cabanas. Sand spilled into his Gucci loafers, and mosquitoes began to find him in a whining haze.

Renard cursed softly, thinking to himself as he watched James Hawker's silhouette in the cabana window. Summer was no time to be in the tropics. Too many bugs. Wilting heat. And it was not unlikely there were snakes, too.

Renard shuddered. Snakes revolted him—as did, in fact, this

entire island. He couldn't keep a crease in his slacks because of the humidity. There was no such thing as room service, because there wasn't a hotel on the whole irritating chunk of sand. Just stone and wood cabins. A resort camp, they called it. Pirate's Point, Little Cayman Island, British West Indies.

He had spent three days there watching Hawker.

He'd done everything properly, too. Just as he always did. Renard was a fanatic about the proprieties of his craft. After a workmanlike job of tailing Hawker to the tropics, he had bugged his room, along with the rooms of that older fellow named Hayes and his surly British butler.

And he had heard just enough to convince him that his employers in New York were correct. Hayes had plans to stick his nose into the business of Fister Corporation. And that simply couldn't be tolerated—not that Renard cared much about Fister Corporation. It was his employer, nothing more. Just as Dubois Ltd. of London occasionally employed him, as did the Galtchen firm of Munich and, once, even the Union Corse of France. Of course, now he did most of his work for Fister Corporation, or the Unione Siciliano.

It made no difference to Renard who paid him. But the proprieties of the craft required a certain loyalty to one's employer.

So, now they all would die, the three of them.

It was easy. Almost too easy. Except for the heat. And the bugs. And this god-damn island. Nothing to do but scuba dive and fish.

Renard had no interest in such things. He had tried scuba diving once. On the clear reef off Bloody Bay. It had been a group dive, with Hawker, Hayes, the butler, and three or four other guests of the resort. It had amused Renard to think that he would soon be killing the three men he accompanied side by side, underwater.

He could have, in fact, killed them then. But there were all those irritating fish down there to worry about. And, of course, the other guests of the resort might see him.

It wouldn't have been a very professional job.

And no matter how distasteful he found the surroundings, he would still do the very best job he could.

Later, though, his return to Miami would be pleasant, Renard thought as he waited. He liked Miami—in the winter.

Since he had established himself with the organization, he had been able to afford to go to Miami for a few weeks every winter. He always took a lady with him. Something attractive, something to complement his own good looks. Like that blonde last winter. Britta? Yes, Britta. Tall blonde with legs a mile long and spectacular mammary development. She was the one with the fake furs and the bright-red lipstick and enough paste diamonds to open her own five-and-ten. They had had some laughs. Won big on the horses at Hialeah, then blew it all—and more—on the dogs in Biscayne.

But when the money was gone, Britta had started getting bitchy. Whining all the time. Sitting in their hotel room polishing her nails, belting down martinis and chainsmoking. Then she started getting unpleasant about that problem he had in bed, laughing at him. She had made the mistake of turning his inabilities against him like a weapon.

Renard's finger twitched nervously on the trigger of the Colt as he thought about it.

The woman had gotten exactly what she deserved. Who in the hell was she to call him a faggot? He didn't accept that kind of talk from anyone—especially a 42nd Street whore.

So he had killed her. Damn right, he had killed her. He had punched her infuriating face to pulp, then gone to work on her throat until he was sure she would never call him another name. Ever.

As Renard relived the hooker's death, his breathing became shallow and the muscles of his face went slack.

He had a hard, dark, bullfighter's face and a thin moustache.

After a time, his eyes fluttered open and his breathing returned to normal. Deep inside, Renard felt the warm, good glow he always felt after he had killed.

It was a feeling better than any other, better than drugs or booze.

When he was younger, that feeling had frightened him. Like after that cat he had played with . . . then tortured . . . then beheaded in secret, way back when he was twelve; just him and the cat in that alleyway near their flat outside Versailles.

Or when he was in his teens and found himself driving alone in his old Fiat, far beyond Paris, and he had seen that horse all by itself in the pasture, looking sleepy in the light of the full moon.

It had frightened him because who in his right mind would butcher a cat or slit a horse's throat just for the hell of it?

It wasn't until much later in his life that he admitted to himself why he did it. It wasn't until he had already eliminated a few people and the organization had hired him and treated him with respect because he was very, very good at what he did.

It was only then that Renard finally admitted to himself that he killed for one reason, and one reason only.

He killed because it made him feel good.

Now killing was his job. His craft, as he liked to think of it. And he had risen very quickly to the top of his field.

He was rare among assassins because he killed intelligently and without mercy. He planned every step of a job meticulously, from his first advance to his final escape.

Renard liked to think that, whatever difficulties a job presented, he had the ingenuity and the intellect to complete it as quietly and discreetly as possible.

Time was rarely a consideration. If an assassination took weeks to set up and effect, then Renard invested weeks. Once he'd worked for a month as an elevator operator before he found the perfect opportunity to make his hit. But his insistence on a perfect kill each and every time had paid great dividends.

Even the Russians had shown their admiration for his work through intermediaries, querying to see if he might be interested in handling a few of their contracts. He had told the intermediary that he considered their interest a great honor and, yes, of course, he would be pleased to work for them.

The assassin took a deep breath and moved soundlessly to within five feet of the window. Hawker hadn't stirred. He still sat beside the lamp, with the book propped up in front of him.

Against the window shade, Hawker's silhouette was unmistakable: the square jaw; hair medium length and mussed; the broken, boxer's nose.

For a moment, Renard considered going inside to do it. He would enjoy it more, doing it face to face. There was more intimacy in that. And, if Hawker was asleep, that would be even better because he could take his time.

But what if he wasn't asleep? What then?

In his entire life, Renard had never feared any man because he knew he held ultimate hole card—he wasn't afraid to kill.

But there was something in James Hawker's face that troubled him. Perhaps even scared him. Hawker had piercing gray-blue eyes that said more than he wasn't afraid to kill. James Hawker's eyes also said he wasn't afraid to die.

It was the one quality Renard lacked.

He decided not to take the chance of confronting Hawker face to face.

Quietly and deliberately, Renard lifted the Colt Detective in both hands to steady the unbalanced weight of the silencer. He brought the fixed sights to bear on Hawker's right temple, then cocked back the hammer.

He held the revolver in place for a full minute, enjoying the sudden godlike power he wielded. When his chest began to heave and his heart began to race high in his throat, he knew it was time. Lovingly, Renard squeezed the trigger.

The little Colt thudded, jumping in his hand. The window shattered as a chunk of cranium exploded from the silhouetted head, and Hawker slumped forward, knocking the book and table lamp into darkness.

For James Hawker, it was the final darkness.

Death.

TWO

Renard exhaled deeply, trembling.

He stood outside Hawker's window for a moment, feeling the warmth move through him like a wave. His toes clawed spasmodically within his shoes.

Finally he tapped a Players cigarette out and lighted it. It had been a clean shot. A little high on the temple, perhaps. The window glass had probably caused a slight change in the bullet's trajectory. But not enough to make any difference.

It had been a clean kill, professionally done. No thrashing and moaning afterward. No time to scream for help.

Hawker never knew what hit him—and that's the only thing Renard regretted.

It would have been nice if he could have looked into Hawker's eyes before he killed him. It would have been much better if he could have looked into his eyes.

When Renard had finished his cigarette, he snuffed it out and jammed the butt into his pocket before he moved on toward the other cabanas to kill Jacob Montgomery Hayes and Hendricks, the Englishman.

Renard decided he wouldn't have to be as careful with these two. With them, he could make it last longer, and enjoy it more.

Afterward, he would escape to Cayman Brac in the boat that Fister Corporation had waiting for him. From there, a company plane would fly him to Miami.

It was an easy job—except for the bugs and the heat. Almost too easy. Renard began to plan the two days he would spend in Miami as he walked toward Hayes's cabana.

He would dine at a good restaurant and flash enough hundred-dollar bills to make the headwaiter jump to light his cigarettes.

Then maybe take in a few races at Hialeah. The corporation had a bookmaker there who would reward him with some winners—as long as he unloaded them on some other bookie.

The corporation was funny about money. They paid royally up front, but they did not like an employee making it through the back door. Renard knew that better than most—it was his job to kill those who tried.

Hayes and Hendricks were in separate cabanas, side by side beneath coconut palms. The orange moon made the coral sand glow like gold along the beach.

Renard walked carefully along the sea's edge, staying in the shadows of the tree line.

Both cabins were dark. Hayes and Hendricks were asleep.

Automatically, Renard tightened the silencer down as he approached the front door of Hayes's cabana and tested the knob.

It wasn't locked, and the door swung open. Renard raised the Colt Detective to fire, then flipped on the overhead light.

The room was empty. The bed was still made.

What is happening? he wondered in French.

As he turned to walk quickly to the next cabana, something whistled out of the darkness and clubbed the gun from his hand. In the same instant, two figures appeared in front of him: the stocky figure of Hayes and the lanky, somber Englishman, Hendricks.

"Renard—catch!" said a voice, and Renard was aware of something tumbling through the moonlight toward his face. He got his hands up just in time to knock it away. In the light from the room, he could see that they had thrown a fish at him; a funny-looking, colorful fish with bright fanlike spines. Renard jerked back involuntarily, kicking at the thing.

"Hey, god damn it, what is the big idea—"

He stopped in midsentence and suddenly grabbed his right hand. Renard looked at the two men, his eyes growing wide. "This fish has stung me or something . . . stings like hell!"

Jacob Montgomery Hayes, who, along with being one of the world's richest men, was also a respected amateur biologist, watched patiently as the blood drained from the assassin's face.

Renard's breathing was already becoming labored.

Calmly Hayes peeled off the heavy rubber gloves he had used to protect his own hands. "You've had a very unlucky holiday, Mr. Renard," he said easily. "You went out for a walk on the beach this evening and made the silly mistake of picking up a scorpionfish—or, at least, that's what the authorities will think."

"M-monsieur!" Renard stammered, still wringing his hands

as if he might somehow be able to scrape the sting away. "The pain is very bad! I will require medical attention if . . . this . . . this . . ."

The assassin's face contorted as his body heaved with flooding pain.

"A doctor wouldn't help, I'm afraid, Mr. Renard," Hayes continued calmly. "There's no known antidote for the sting of a scorpionfish. Ah, from the look on your face, I'd judge the poison is already into your bloodstream. Quite painful, is it? Yes, I've read that it is. Soon you'll begin to experience nausea. Then vomiting. Probably convulsions, too—before you die."

Renard took two painful steps toward Hayes and Hendricks, his hands outstretched. "Please . . ." he sobbed, "you must help me . . . can't stand it . . . I did not want to kill your friend. They made me; the organization made me. Please . . . please . . . I don't want to die . . . God, *the pain!*"

Renard buckled over, clutching his stomach in agony as Hayes allowed himself a thin smile. "I know your record, Renard, and I know the kind of mercy you've shown others. But you have us wrong if you think this is some kind of revenge for the murder of James Hawker." Hayes turned and looked into the darkness. "Is it, James?"

James Hawker stepped out of the shadows of a massive bayonet plant, holstering his customized .45 ACP. "I've got to hand it to you, Jacob," said Hawker as he stood over the writhing figure of Renard. "I think you've just staged the perfect murder."

"The credit goes to Hendricks," Hayes said simply. He looked at his butler and old friend. "One of your tricks from the old days in British Intelligence, right, Hank?"

"Quite, sir," the Englishman said without emotion. "Of course, the plaster bust of James was something less than innovative. But the business with the fish has its novel aspects. The lads at M-5 HQ dreamed it up. Seemed silly at the time—not many scorpionfish around in Verdun or Berlin, you know. But it's actually quite useful in these climes. Unfortunately, though, it's not failsafe."

"Why's that?" demanded Hawker.

Hendricks sniffed. "The sting of a scorpionfish is fatal in about ninety percent of cases where medical attention is not available. Death is likely, but not guaranteed."

Renard was lost in a series of wracking convulsions now. Hawker pocketed the Colt Detective and grabbed the collar of the assassin's coat. "I'm going to do the world a favor and drag this French lunatic down to the water. That ought to finish him." He looked at Hayes. "Maybe you ought to bring that nasty little fish of yours along, Jacob. We don't want to leave it too far from the body. Everything else has been taken care of, right?"

"Right, James. Hendricks found the tapes in Renard's room. He took those and nothing else. I've told Samuel McCoy, the manager, we'll be flying out tonight. From here, we'll be flying to Grand Cayman where you'll let me off."

"Why Grand Cayman?"

"There were two reasons for my coming to the islands—" A light smile crossed his lips. "—aside from the bonefishing, I mean. One, I wanted to show you just how professional and how thorough the Fister Corporation is. I think Renard amply demonstrated that. He tailed you from the moment I put you on the case—and I have no idea how they found out we were interested in their New York scam.

"Two, since the late sixties, Grand Cayman has become one of the great tax havens of the western world. There are four hundred nineteen banks on Grand Cayman, and all just as tight-lipped as any bank Switzerland has to offer. If you want to hide illegal earnings, or set up dupe corporations, Grand Cayman is the place to do it. Fister Corporation is both registered and licensed in Grand Cayman, so if I'm to do my job—"

"I'll still not even sure what *my* job is," Hawker interrupted.

Hayes smiled. "You will, Hawk. I'll tell you all about it tonight on the plane. Believe me, I didn't call you down here just to fly fish for bones."

Renard had settled into a series of convulsions, followed by a moaning catatonia. Hawker dragged him through the sand and dropped him facedown into the water. The assassin choked violently, then looked up through a haze of pain. His eyes seemed to focus, then refocus on Hawker's face.

"But you are . . . you are *dead*," Renard hissed.

James Hawker turned and didn't look back.

"Let's not spread it around, Renard," he said. "You're the only one who knows."

THREE

The plane Jacob Hayes kept in the Caymans was a three-engine Trislander he had outfitted with bunks and a tiny kitchenette for long trips. The flight from Little Cayman to Grand Cayman, however, took less than an hour, so the three men sat forward.

Hendricks flew the plane, so his boss, Hayes, could be free to explain the mission to Hawker.

It was Hawker's fourth mission under the alliance he and Hayes had formed. The premise of the alliance was that crime in the United States was raging out of control. Conventional police forces had their hands tied by ridiculous laws that protected the criminal and said, in effect, to hell with the victims. Hayes looked upon the law enforcement/judicial system as a symptom of social softness. And, as a biologist, he knew that when any species lost the instinct to justly protect itself, that species condemned itself to extinction.

Hawker, who had been Chicago's most decorated cop before he resigned out of disgust, had seen too many good arrests thrown out of court on legal technicalities not to agree.

So, the alliance had been formed. Hayes, a multibillionaire, would provide the funding. Hawker would provide the skills and firepower. Their goal: to go wherever they were needed to teach people how to fight for themselves.

Under the alliance, Hawker had collided head on with revolutionaries in Florida, savage street gangs in L.A., and I.R.A. renegades in Chicago.

Now he was ready for his fourth mission.

More than ready.

As they flew over the *Mar Caribe*—the Caribbean Sea—Hawker reflected on the months of inactivity he had suffered beneath the winter skies of Chicago. He had stayed in shape all right. His daily workout of calisthenics and running would have tested a Spartan, and he maintained his boyhood habit of boxing at the old Bridgeport gym. To improve his computer pirating skills, he had even taken an advanced programing course at the Chicago campus of the University of Illinois.

Even so, the inactivity had taken its toll.

He had felt listless, even depressed. He couldn't help thinking about the I.R.A. mission and the sister he had never met until moments before she died.

He had no trouble keeping off body fat, but in that last month of inactivity, he could almost feel his fighting instincts growing soft from neglect.

So now he had a mission again, and it felt good.

Damn good.

He sat behind Hendricks, who handled the controls of the sleek Trislander stoically and professionally. Hawker was anxious for Hayes to begin, but he made a point not to show his eagerness.

Hayes would get around to it when he was ready. Hayes had

a reason for everything he did. Like Hawker, he was a methodical man. In their three days together on Little Cayman, Hayes had been uncommunicative. On the first day, wading the flats for bonefish, Hayes had told him briefly that he had ordered Hawker to New York for a reason, and from New York to the islands for a reason.

He told him he would discover the reasons soon enough.

Other than discussing their plans to handle Renard, Hayes seemed satisfied to spend their days together concentrating on the flats fish and the landlocked tarpon available to any fly fisherman lucky enough to visit Little Cayman.

Flying at a comfortable 2500 feet, they could see how moonlight turned the expanse of Caribbean Sea into an ice field of cobalt and satin. The gauge lights of the plane were lime green, and they softly illuminated the bony face of Hendricks and the thick, no-nonsense face of Hayes.

Finally, Hayes put away the logbook he had been updating, adjusted his wire-rimmed glasses, then twisted around in his seat to face Hawker.

"So," he said, "what did you think of Renard?"

Hawker shrugged. "A professional. In the three days he was on the island, I never caught him staring at me once. He plausibly played the role of the wealthy French playboy on a get-away vacation. I had no idea he was following me until I arrived and you filled me in a little on Fister Corporation and some of the people it employed. He did a good job bugging our apartments. Now I understand why you didn't want me to destroy the bugs—it would have tipped our hand." Hawker thought for a moment. "Renard's one mistake was underestimating us."

"Right," Hayes interjected. "And let's hope they keep underestimating us." He searched through his flight jacket momentarily, then produced his heavy briar pipe. Noticing the way Hendricks wrinkled his nose, Hayes tamped the pipe full of tobacco but did not light it.

"Hawk, I had you go to New York because I wanted you to familiarize yourself with the area—specifically, The Bronx. That's also why I went ahead and sent your equipment there—all you have to do is call for it at the warehouse."

Hawker nodded. He had spent four days in The Bronx, learning the streets, meeting a few people. On Jacob's orders, he had leased a flat not far from Yankee Stadium and made arrangements with a storage concern before he flew to Little Cayman.

"That part of The Bronx looks like a war zone, I know," Hayes continued. "But lately there have been sporadic efforts at reclamation. Now, for a variety of reasons, a large federal grant has been authorized. The money will be used for the construction of huge apartment complexes and office towers in what was once a thriving ethnic German neighborhood of about thirty square blocks. One edge of that neighborhood is about twenty-five blocks from a still prosperous section of The Bronx, and the federal government hopes that the redevelopment of the German neighborhood will gradually lead to the reclamation of the connecting territory. Following me so far?"

Hawker nodded and said nothing.

"Good." Hayes removed the pipe from his teeth, using it to emphasize his next point. "A project of this magnitude means that canny and often corrupt developers and landlords can make fortunes. One of the largest development corporations in the city is owned by Fister Corporation, under the name Fister Limited.

"Now, Fister Corporation, you see, has a history of obscuring its scale and worth by working through numerous wholly owned subsidiaries. Through bribery and maybe some blackmail, Fister Corporation learned almost a year ago of this federal grant for The Bronx. As a result, its subsidiaries have been buying up just as much of the neighborhood as it can. Because most of this area consists of junked lots or abandoned buildings, it was easy for them to buy fast and cheap. But the remaining, oh, five or ten percent of the neighborhood consists of brownstone houses in which live some tough and stubborn old German families. And Hawk, if those Germans wouldn't move when The Bronx was going to hell around them, they sure as hell don't plan to move now that the place is going to be fixed up."

"Is that the conflict?" Hawker put in. "Fister Corporation wants to buy, but the Germans don't want to sell?"

Hayes smiled. "Exactly. It's not an uncommon situation in the world of urban reclamation. But Fister Corporation has, unfortunately, uncommon ways of dealing with it." Hayes raised his eyebrows and looked into Hawker's eyes. "Renard is a perfect example of their methods. Very professional. Very cold. And absolutely without mercy."

"Then they've already chased the Germans out?"

Hendricks allowed himself a rare chuckle. "Jacob, permit me to explain to James about the Germans—he's obviously too young to remember much about World War II."

Hawker listened with a wry expression on his face while the Englishman straightened him out.

"You must remember," Hendricks went on, "that the Germans—using the resources of a country only the size of your Georgia—came all too close to defeating the entire world in a highly complex, highly mechanized war. Thumb your nose all you like at the taboo subject of racial traits, but the fact is, the Germanic tribes do not frighten easily." The old Englishman chuckled softly. "Jerry gave us all quite a turn back in those days. Quite."

"I stand corrected," Hawker allowed. "The German families have *not* been chased out of The Bronx."

"Less than sixty families remain," continued Hayes. "And they're having a tough time of it. The head of Fister Corporation is Blake Fister. He achieved prominence in the tough world of New York real estate by the almost indiscriminate use of corruption and intimidation. From there, he pyramided his holdings into a billion-dollar international conglomerate. But he still keeps a firm hand on the home operation. He considers its continued success a matter of personal pride. If he somehow got beaten on his own home turf, Fister would lose no little esteem among his fellows in the world of international finance. And no one is more aware of this than Blake Fister.

"In the last month, the German families have been subjected to increasing pressure in the forms of threatening phone calls and personal attacks disguised as street muggings. To carry out his dirty work, Fister employs a Mafia organization of about twenty-two individuals who specialize in strong-arm tactics and murder."

Hawker had grown increasingly interested as he listened. "Renard was from his security force?"

"Renard, according to my sources, is among the elite of the world's professional assassins. He contracts out and works totally alone. And, as I said, he is a fair example of what we can expect if we choose to butt heads with Fister."

"What about the New York cops? Aren't they doing anything about it?" Hawker asked.

"I suspect the precinct police are sympathetic but powerless. They have a suspicion about what's going on, but they lack the manpower and money it would take to get evidence."

Hawker stretched in his seat. The bright holiday glow of Grand Cayman Island was just ahead in the pitch of black sea, and Hendricks nosed the plane down as he started his descent toward Owen Roberts International Airport.

"And you think you can get the necessary evidence here?" Hawker said.

"With a little luck, I can." Hayes smiled. "I own four of the island's four hundred banks, and that will be a start."

Hawker returned his smile. "And I suppose I am to go on to New York and start sniffing around, try to organize the German families?"

As the plane touched, skidded, and screeched on the cement runway, Hayes clapped James Hawker on the back. "More than that, Hawk—much more than that. One man can't beat Fister Corporation, no matter how tough he is. I need you to come up with some kind of master plan so we can hit this bastard from more than one side. Use me. Use Hendricks. Hell, hire the New York National Guard if they'll go for it—but get the job done."

Jacob Montgomery Hayes stood and got his nylon duffel

bag from behind the seat as Hendricks swung open the door. Just before he exited into the balmy Caribbean night, he added, "And don't forget, Hawk—they know about us. Renard was proof of that. They'll be gunning for you. And they're going to throw the very best the criminal underworld has to offer right at your head. . . ."

FOUR

Little Cayman (Sunrise)

From the distance of his back porch, Samuel McCoy, manager of Pirates' Point Lodge, thought the figure on the beach was the corpse of a bottle-nosed dolphin.

Occasionally a dolphin would fall victim to one of the great rogue sharks of the open sea. Samuel had grown up in the Caymans, and he knew such things happen.

He finished his coffee, smiled at his wife, Mary, as he slid the cup onto the counter, then turned and walked barefoot toward the turquoise sea.

As he neared the beach, he hesitated, confused.

The figure was not that of a dolphin, he realized. It was a man. A man dressed in a blue leisure suit. The man lay half in the water, his face a chalky white, looking skyward.

Samuel began to run. He splashed into the surf beside the body and grabbed the man by the shoulders and pulled him out onto the beach. He recognized the man immediately: a guest, a Frenchman who had registered under the name of LeBlac and paid cash in advance.

As Samuel had told his old friend Jacob Hayes, there was something about this Frenchman he did not like. Something about the man he did not trust.

As he ripped the Frenchman's shirt away to check for a heartbeat, something high on the surfline caught his eye. Something no one but an old Caymanian would have noticed. It was the bloated carcass of a small, multicolored fish.

A scorpionfish.

Samuel immediately checked the man's feet. He was wearing shoes.

But then he saw the Frenchman's right hand, and he knew. The hand was swollen to three times its normal size, and bright-red rays traced their way up his arm, disappearing beneath the sleeve of his jacket.

As Samuel bent to check the man's pulse, he heard a scream of surprise. He turned to see his wife running toward him. She was a handsome, nut-brown woman of Indian descent, and she ran heavily.

"Oh, Samuel! What has happened? Is he . . . is he . . ."

Samuel McCoy held his wife, calming her. "He picked up a scorpionfish, I guess. Not much we can do about it now, Mary. No need getting upset." He looked at the Frenchman and shrugged. "I'm just sorry it had to happen here—"

He stopped in midsentence, his eyes frozen on the body. Had it moved?

Immediately he dropped to his knees and pressed his ear against the Frenchman's chest. The beat was so frail, he couldn't be sure. He touched the man's neck and held his ear close to the Frenchman's mouth, hoping to feel the slight warmth of exhalation.

But instead, he heard a distant garbled whisper. A single word. A word more like a groan. It seemed to originate within the very bowels of the assassin, like an oath.

Hawker . . .

Samuel McCoy's eyes grew wide. "Mary!" he said quickly. "Go for help. Now! Call Cayman Brae for a doctor!"

"Oh, thank God," she said out loud as she ran back to the lodge. "Thank God he is alive. . . ."

FIVE

New York City

To the passengers aboard the Trans World Airlines 747, the setting sun seemed to transform the endless gray canyons of the city into an inferno of molten steel and blazing glass.

James Hawker stared out his porthole window in first class and forced himself to ignore the fiery light that bathed the Statue of Liberty, the United Nations Building, and all the other landmarks associated with New York.

Instead, he made himself memorize the area as he would a topographical map: a field of battle.

Manhattan was a thin island jammed between the Hudson River and the East River. To the east were the endless crackerbox suburbs of Queens. Brooklyn was a haze of industrial smog to the south that seemed to extend far out into the Atlantic. To the north, separated from Manhattan by the narrow Harlem River, was The Bronx—a wasteland of slums, broken industry, and bleak brownstone houses.

Satisfied he had the geographical chunks fixed in his mind, Hawker settled back and relaxed as the 747 seemed to gain speed, locked down its landing gear, and roared earthward toward the cement expanse of LaGuardia.

After an hour of baggage lines and surly people, Hawker exited the airport. The night was oily with heat and smog.

Outside LaGuardia, the shuttle buses and private cars were bumper to bumper, blaring at each other.

Hawker walked to the first yellow cab in line and tapped the driver on the shoulder. The driver was black and he wore an ornate western hat. He lowered the tout sheet he was reading.

"I don't go to no Yonkers or Mount Vernon," the driver said immediately. "And I don't carry no bags."

"You're in luck," said Hawker as he opened the back door and slid his duffel bag in. "The Bronx. Rhinestrauss Avenue. You know it?"

"Shi-i-i-t." The driver smiled. "I growed up not ten blocks from there." As he started the meter and jammed the car into gear, he looked over his shoulder at Hawker. "What I want to know, mister man, is why a dude like you wants to go to that shithole? I know a fine hotel up near Fordham I could take you. Plenty college girls, 'case you get lonely—"

"I'm going to Rhinestrauss," Hawker interrupted. "I'm trying to broaden my horizons."

Hawker settled back, amused. Visiting New York was like a trip into limbo, a maze of the lonely, the aloof, and the mad.

Everyone in New York was on the make. They always had an angle. The driver undoubtedly got some kind of kickback from the hotel near Fordham he had mentioned. And he probably had the same deal with a couple of prostitutes there who specialized in posing as coeds.

Hawker decided it would be an interesting city in which to live. But he sure as hell didn't treasure visiting there.

Once behind the wheel, the driver was transformed from a hotel tout into a grand-prix enthusiast. He tailgated. He rode his brakes. He pounded on his horn and shouted out loud as he needled his taxi in and out of traffic.

They roared down Grand Central Parkway to Route 278 and the causeway over Ward's Island. Traffic was heavy into The Bronx, but the driver made good time—not that Hawker was interested in making good time.

Finally he tapped on the bulletproof glass that separated the front of the cab from the back.

The driver slid open the little door without slowing down. "What'cha need, buddy?"

"I need you to quit driving like your wife has big insurance policies on both of us."

"My wife?" The driver flashed a grin of bad teeth. "Shit, man, she ain't got no insurance on nothin'. It's just that some dudes behind us either followin' us or want to race."

Hawker glanced back over his shoulder. A black Lincoln Continental with tinted windows was right on their bumper.

"How long have they been there?"

"Since we left fuckin' LaGuardia, man." The driver seemed to see Hawker for the first time. He said, "You look like the kind'a guy what's got some enemies, huh?"

"Maybe," said Hawker. "First chance you get, hit the brakes. Make them pass."

The driver seemed glad for the excitement. "You got it, mister man. Hang onto your B.V.D's."

The two cars roared over the bridge and down Ward's Island's main road doing sixty. On the first open straightaway, the driver punched the taxi into passing gear, then immediately hit the brakes. The Continental skidded behind them, just missed their back bumper, and swerved past.

"Now," said Hawker, "just do the speed limit and see if they try to get behind us again."

The Lincoln raced on ahead, then turned suddenly onto a side street. As the taxi slowed for the toll booth near Downing Stadium, Hawker realized the Continental had gone around the block.

"They on our ass again," the driver said, looking in the mirror.

"Yeah," said Hawker. "I see that. We're not too far from Rhinestrauss Avenue, are we?"

"What's the address?"

Hawker told him.

"Shit, man, that's the fucking slums! Ain't nothing in that area but old wornout factories, retired krauts, and Puerto Rican niggers."

"Don't worry about what's there. How long before we get to it?"

The black man touched the brim of his hat. He looked concerned. "Maybe ten, maybe fifteen minutes."

"Fine. But instead of driving straight there, I want you to drop me off on the backside of the block. Can you do that?"

"Hell, yes, I *can* do it. But look, mister, you just a fare to me. I didn't sign on for no *Dukes of Hazzard* show. I done been through Korea. I don't need this shit."

Hawker folded a twenty-dollar bill and slid it through the little window. "You get another one when we get there. Okay?"

The driver checked the bill and jammed it into his pocket. "Hell, I do damn near anything for forty, mister man. Long as I don't have to kill nobody."

"Don't worry," Hawker said easily. "I'll take care of that."

The driver began to giggle, but stopped abruptly when he realized that Hawker wasn't kidding.

Hawker unzipped his duffel bag and unholstered the .45 Colt Commander he had had customized by the artists at Devel Corporation. He had had them add a wide-grip safety and a Bo-Mar rear sight, as well as increase the clip capacity along with some other shooting niceties.

He had had no trouble getting the handgun back through Miami customs because he and Hendricks had flown the dark eastern corridor over Cuba to the States alone, in the Trislander.

The customs men had simply nodded at their sparse luggage and sent them on their way. At Miami International Airport, Hawker had checked his bag through to New York at the TWA counter, while Hendricks made arrangements to have the Trislander stored.

On their trip to Miami, Hawker and the old English butler had discussed a couple of scenarios for getting at Fister Corporation. Hawker's ideas tended to be more direct. Hendricks's plans leaned toward the oblique and outre.

Even so, Hawker respected the butler's intellect and British Intelligence training immensely.

Finally they settled on a combination of two ideas.

So, with an unemotional "good luck" and "safe journey," Hendricks had flown off to London, while Hawker took TWA to New York.

Hawker had expected action, but he hadn't planned on having to use his Colt Commander so soon.

From his duffel bag, he took one of the eight-round clips and fixed it snug into the grip. Then he slid a round into the chamber and locked in the safety.

Hawker glanced out the rear window. The Lincoln was staying a more conservative distance behind them now, trying to blend into the darkness and the traffic.

Through the hole in the glass partition, Hawker ordered, "Put some more distance between us. When we get to the back side of Rhinestrauss, I want to get out without being seen. After I'm gone, I want you to circle around and stop in front of the address I gave you, as if you'd just let me out. Got it?"

The driver looked offended. "I look dumb or something to you, mister? Hell, yes, I got it—but I ain't doing a thing till I get me that other twenty."

Hawker smiled and settled back. He wore a dark-blue Cuban shirt and white deck pants. He considered changing out of the pants into something less visible.

He decided not to bother.

The driver raced north on the Bronx River Parkway, then swung off abruptly on the Gun Hill Road exit. Five blocks later, he made a quick right, then a quicker left. He skidded to a halt and threw open the door.

"Your address is straight through those houses," he said, pointing. "I'll pull around there just like you said—but I got to hurry. The Lincoln ain't far behind."

Hawker stuffed the second twenty in the man's hand, grabbed his duffel bag, and slammed the door.

The driver grinned as he skidded away, yelling, "Good luck, buddy. You'll be lucky if you don't get mugged before those dudes in the Lincoln catch you!"

Hawker disappeared into the shadows just before the Lincoln squealed around the corner. He watched the limousine follow the taxi down the block, then turn west toward Rhinestrauss Avenue.

Hawker made his way down an alley squeezed between two deserted tenements. Someone had strung across a chain-link fence and posted a city proclamation of condemnation.

Hawker vaulted over the fence and sprinted toward the street where, between two somber brownstones, he could see the taxi slowing. He got to Rhinestrauss just before the Lincoln did.

He stood in the shadows, waiting.

The black taxi driver made a show of slamming the trunk shut—as if Hawker had just exited into the brownstone across the street.

The Lincoln slowed behind the taxi, then stopped.

Hawker assumed the men inside would wait until the taxi was gone, then go into the brownstone, looking for him. He planned to follow them in and take them from behind.

He didn't want any gunplay—not this soon. Hopefully, he would be able to take them alive and slap some information out of them before turning them over to the cops.

But Hawker's assumptions were all wrong.

The men in the Lincoln didn't wait until the taxi had pulled away.

Instead, three of the four doors swung open, and the men who exited stood facing the taxi driver.

The three of them wore dark suits, with hats pulled down low on their heads. All held automatic weapons.

Hawker watched the taxi driver's face tighten. "What the hell you dudes think you're doin', pointing them guns at me?" he bluffed, putting on a brave front.

"Where is he?" one of the men demanded.

"If you mean that dude I just brung from LaGuardia, he done went into that there house. I don't know nothin' more."

"You're lying!" the man snapped. "Where'd you let him off?"

The taxi driver tilted his hat back on his head. "It's just like I told you, mister man—"

Hawker thought they'd give him one more chance to tell the truth. He thought they might grab him and slap him around—and, by that time, he would be in position.

It was Hawker's second lesson in Fister Corporation diplomacy.

The three men didn't wait. They opened fire at once. Their weapons were outfitted with silencers. The silencers made the automatics sound like hydraulic staple guns.

The taxi driver jolted backward into his taxi, slapping at the slugs as they plowed into his body.

The three men moved toward the driver as they fired. It gave Hawker the opening he was looking for. The Colt was a fine handgun, but he had to be within fifteen yards of his targets to do any kind of sharpshooting.

Hawker sprinted toward the back of the car, hoping to take cover there.

He had almost made it, when one of the Fister Corporation's three hit men saw him. The man swung his automatic around, firing. Asphalt at Hawker's heels screamed behind him.

Hawker dove headlong onto the street behind the Lincoln.

He could hear the shoe leather slap as the men ran toward him. He rolled beneath the car and fired at the first set of legs he saw.

A man swore violently and collapsed on the street, rolling over and over in agony, holding his right shin.

Hawker immediately popped up and squeezed off two shots in rapid fire. A second man gave a hideous scream and pressed a hand to the gore that was now his face.

He fell to the earth and kicked his legs wildly for a moment, then lay still.

The third man released a long burst of fire, and Hawker ducked for cover again.

He looked beneath the car—just in time. The third man, following Hawker's lead, had dropped to his belly, trying to get a shot at Hawker's legs.

Hawker didn't hesitate. With one long stride, he jumped onto the trunk of the car as slugs sprayed the asphalt. But, instead of stopping on the trunk, Hawker ran up over the roof of the car and down onto the hood.

As Fister Corporation's hit man struggled to his feet, the Colt Commander jumped twice in Hawker's big right hand.

The man was slammed backward onto the pavement, as if his legs had been chopped from under him.

His head hit with a terrible thud, and he did not stir.

The left lapel of his jacket began to glisten with black seepage from the two holes in his heart.

Hawker jumped down from the car and walked toward the man he had shot in the leg. The man's automatic—a 9mm

Uzi, Hawker could see now—had been knocked away when he was hit.

Now the man was crawling toward his weapon.

He left a bright trail of blood on the street.

Calmly Hawker kicked the weapon even farther, away. The man looked up. He had a pinched, feral face and dark eyes.

"Don't kill me," he pleaded. "Please don't kill me. I been hit. I been hit bad."

The man held his leg and groaned, as if to prove it was in bad shape.

Hawker stood above him, with the stainless-steel Colt pointed at the man's head. "Talk to me," he whispered between tight lips. "Who sent you? How did you know I was coming?"

The man shook his head violently. "I don't know nothing . . . can't even think. The pain's too bad. . . ."

Hawker dropped to one knee. He grabbed the man's shirt collar and shook him. "Renard was sent to the Caribbean to kill me. How did you people know he didn't? Damn it, talk! You won't get another chance."

The man's face contorted as if in great pain. "For God's sake, leave me alone," he moaned. "I don't know nothing. I just do what they tell me."

"Who's *they?*" Hawker demanded. "Blake Fister? Did he send you?"

The sudden change in the man's expression told Hawker that Blake Fister had, indeed, sent him.

The man rolled away from him and huddled against the pavement.

Hawker snorted in disgust. How in the hell had they known

he was coming? Hawker wondered. Samuel McCoy was an old friend of Jacob Montgomery Hayes, and he certainly wouldn't have tipped off the Fister people.

And Renard was dead . . . or was he?

Hawker remembered what Hendricks had said about the scorpionfish being fatal 90 percent of the time when the victim received no medical attention. But Hawker had pulled the French assassin into the water himself.

Even if the poison hadn't killed him, he would have certainly drowned. . . .

As Hawker lost himself in thought, he momentarily lowered the Colt.

It was a mistake.

The wounded man's right hand was a blur as it arced toward Hawker's face. The stiletto glimmer of steel told him, in that slow-motion microsecond, that the man had drawn a knife as he huddled close to the pavement.

Hawker got his left hand up just in time. He caught the man's wrist and diverted the power stroke away from his body, into the pavement.

Hawker clubbed the man twice in the face with the back of his right fist, but lost control of the knife in the struggle.

With a final effort, the man swung the knife at him again. Hawker managed to knock it away, then put all of his weight behind an overhand right that crushed the man's throat closed.

The man gagged and floundered on the pavement, clawing at his own face, desperate for air.

Hawker stood away from him and watched as the man's face

slowly darkened, turning blue. The man gave a final convulsive heave, then lay still.

Hawker retrieved the Colt he had dropped in the struggle. He weighed it reflectively in his hand, then looked around at the silent black Lincoln, the taxi, and the four corpses.

When the taxi driver had been shot, he had fallen back into the cab. The door of the cab was open, and the dome light showed the driver's face as a black mask frozen in pain.

Hawker noticed there were more lights on in the row of brownstone houses now. People peeked out from behind curtains.

In the distance, he could hear the anxious scream of sirens.

James Hawker shook his head wearily.

Shit, he whispered.

SIX

Detective Lieutenant Scott Callis usually worked undercover. He worked narcotics, homicide, and sometimes even vice.

But tonight, he was on conventional duty, working the streets.

Like all the other precincts in The Bronx, the Pelham Station was overworked and understaffed. Their precinct was a war zone, ripe with teenage thugs, lunatic rapists, and professional crooks, murderers, and hookers.

The one place they rarely had trouble in was the Rhinestrauss Avenue section, an area of older German immigrants.

But lately, even the Germans had been getting their share—and Callis had a good idea why. Like tonight. A hysterical call about gunshots and multiple homicides on Rhinestrauss.

If it was true, it might be time to do some serious checking. He had heard the street talk, and he knew a little bit about Fister Corporation.

But rumors were one thing, and proof was something else.

It took time to get evidence. It took time and money and

manpower—luxuries his precinct didn't have. Pelham Station was little more than a fort among savages, and few cops lasted more than a year or two there.

But Callis had lasted.

Callis had lasted eight years, going on nine. And in his years, he had seen every brand of crooked scheme, every form of human suffering.

The years had taken their toll. Callis had been shot once, stabbed three times, and, bizarrely, he had been infected with gonorrhea after being bitten and scratched by a Gun Hill whore.

Of the five wounds, the gonorrhea had been the most difficult to explain to his wife.

Now his ex-wife.

Like most cops who worked violent crime, he was divorced.

Callis was a third-generation New Yorker of Greek immigrant stock. He had the wavy black hair, the prominent nose, and thick stature of most men from the ancient island. He was 5' 10" and weighed 195, with wide shoulders and massive olive-tinted hands.

As he forced his unmarked car, with siren blaring, through the 10 P.M. traffic, he touched his sports jacket mechanically to make sure his weapon was there.

It was. A stainless Smith & Wesson .357 in a quick-release holster.

Out of all the cops in America, fewer than eight percent ever had to draw their guns and fire in earnest.

But all the cops in America didn't work Pelham Station.

In his eight years, Callis had already been forced to shoot six men. Four of them had died.

Callis turned right onto Rhinestrauss and skidded in behind the patrol car from which now exited two uniformed cops.

Three bodies lay in the street in plain sight. Blood had pooled beneath them, black as oil in the white glare of the street's vapor lights.

A fourth body was thrown over the seat of a yellow cab.

Callis paused while he called in his location, carefully surveying the area to make sure some lunatic wasn't waiting to drop him the moment he stepped from his vehicle.

Finally he drew the Smith & Wesson, got out of his car, and left the door open.

SEVEN

In the five minutes before the cops arrived, James Hawker tested and discarded a number of plausible lies to tell them.

Finally he decided just to tell the truth.

Some of the truth, anyway.

When the two squad cars arrived, Hawker left his Colt on the hood of the Lincoln and held his hands out to show that he was unarmed. He felt sheepish and disgusted.

This was exactly the kind of trouble he wanted to avoid—especially at the beginning of a mission. But it had happened, and he would have to deal with it.

The first two cops were uniformed. Stupidly, they both jumped out of their car before they even took time to draw their weapons. Had the situation been different, they both could have been blown away before they had a chance to reconsider.

The third cop was a plainclothesman. Hawker noted that he handled himself carefully and professionally. Hawker ignored the rapid-fire questions of the two uniformed cops and waited for the detective to arrive.

The detective approached slowly, then stopped two body lengths in front of Hawker. He held the stainless .357 skyward, but ready.

"What's your name?"

Hawker told him.

"Did you kill these men?"

Hawker nodded. "The three guys in suits, I killed. They killed the taxi driver."

"Why?"

"They were trying to kill me."

"Real bad boys, huh? They just up and decided to kill you? Or maybe you just up and decided to kill them."

"Before I say anything else . . .?"

"The name's Callis. Detective Lieutenant." The Greek cop's eyes never wavered from Hawker's as he spoke. Hawker knew the look. He had handled himself the same way once upon a time; a million years ago, it seemed, when he had worked the streets of Chicago. Callis was carefully surveying him and the situation. And from that look, Hawker knew that Callis wouldn't hesitate to blow his head off if need be.

"Before I say anything else, Detective Callis," Hawker continued calmly, "why don't you have these two guys holster their weapons." Hawker held his hands out again, slowly. "If you look closely, you'll see I'm unarmed. And after watching the Chinese fire drill they put on getting out of their squad car, I just don't feel comfortable with their pointing thirty-eights at me."

"You don't give the orders around here," one of the cops hissed, taking a step toward Hawker.

Callis stopped him with a look. He gave Hawker a long stare

of appraisal, then nodded slowly. "Where's your piece? The one you used to waste these guys?"

Hawker motioned with his head, but did not move his hands. "On the hood of the pimpmobile."

The detective motioned with his .357. "Davis, spread the guy against the squad car and frisk him."

When Davis had finished, Callis nodded, his eyes still locked on Hawker. "Okay, boys. Put your guns away. The guy's right, I'm afraid. I'm going to have to have a long talk with you when we get back to the station about how to approach a hot zone."

"God damn it, Scott," one of the uniforms complained, "we were in a hurry. Hell, a few seconds can save a life—"

"And some day you're going to hurry yourselves right into the grave," Callis snapped. "Now holster your weapons! Davis, you go check the four stiffs. Make sure one of them isn't still breathing. Then call for the forensic boys. I want a lab truck down here pronto. And O'Connor, read this guy his rights before you say another word."

Hawker waited patiently while the cop recited legalese from a plastic card. When he had finished, Callis took a half step closer. "What did you say your name was again?" he snapped.

"Hawker. James Hawker."

Callis touched the black stubble of beard on his thick jaw. "Why is it that name sounds familiar?"

The New York detective was playing staredown as he talked. Hawker didn't flinch. "It's a common name," he answered.

For a moment, a troubled look crossed Callis's face, as if he were struggling to remember something. But then the look passed, and he nodded shrewdly. "Common name, huh? Well,

Hawker, I'm not so sure. I'm not so sure at all. But we'll find out soon enough when I get an N.C.I. check on you. Right now, though, I'm more interested in hearing about how you happened to blow away four guys—"

"Three," Hawker interrupted wryly. "As I told you, I just shot the three guys in suits."

"Ah, that's right," Callis went on with studied sarcasm. "Are you getting this down, O'Connor? This guy is waiving his right to remain silent, and he's admitted to murdering the three stiffs in suits." His head swung back suddenly toward Hawker. "What is it, you got a thing about suits? You don't like guys who wear coats and ties?"

Hawker looked pointedly at Callis's worn sports jacket. "I have noticed that a coat and tie seems to be an advertisement for assholes, but that's not the reason—"

"There you have it, O'Connor," Callis cut in. "We've got a real Bellevue candidate here. A regular Son of Sam." Callis smiled thinly. "So how many more people have you murdered, Hawker? Confession's good for the soul, you know. Just these four? Or maybe you've got a long list stashed away someplace back in your apartment. The world's full of men who wear suits."

Hawker knew what Callis was doing. It was a sophisticated interrogation technique, where patter was used both to relax and confuse the person being questioned.

But Hawker was in no mood for it. "Look, Callis," he said, "if you want your questions answered, I'll answer them. But I'm getting a little tired of your ping-pong talk. If you want to be clever to impress O'Connor here, go right ahead. I'll just wait until you have to wake up a judge to have an attorney appointed for me before I say another word." Hawker returned Callis's thin smile. "I don't mean to offend you, Callis. But I think it'll save us both some time if we understand each other."

Callis actually chuckled. He chuckled softly. He calmly returned the .357 to its shoulder holster, brushed an imaginary piece of lint from his jacket—then, in a blur, grabbed Hawker by the shirt and forced his face down against the squad car.

"You listen, and listen good, smartass," Callis hissed into Hawker's ear. "Because I want to be real sure we do understand each other. You come into my precinct and waste four guys right out on the street, right in plain sight. That upsets people, Hawker. It upsets the citizens in this shithole, and it upsets me. Furthermore, you pick a night when the heat off the streets makes this place as hot as cheerleader's bike seat, and that upsets me even more. You may find this hard to believe, Hawker, but I'd rather be back at the station house sitting in front of a fan and scoring my own farts. I don't like people getting killed in my precinct, Hawker. And I especially don't like the people who do the killing. So, if you don't mind, I'll handle this interrogation any damn way I choose." Callis released Hawker and stepped away. "Now," he said, "do we understand each other a little better?"

Hawker straightened his shirt. "You've got a way with words, Callis." He smiled. "I admire that. And I think we're going to get along fine."

Callis's face tightened for a moment, but then he snorted and wiped his mouth, as if to cover a grin. "Okay, Hawker. Have it your way. No more—what was it? Ping-pong talk? Yeah, ping-pong. I like that. No more ping-pong talk. Just turn around nice and easy while Officer O'Connor puts the cuffs on you and escorts you back to my car."

Hawker was genuinely surprised. "You're arresting me already, Callis? What's the charge?"

Detective Lieutenant Callis straightened his jacket and walked away. He said over his shoulder, "How about murder? Four counts. In the first degree."

EIGHT

London

Hendricks wore a charcoal-gray suit, vest, and bowler hat as he walked down Baker Street toward Westminster.

It had misted rain only an hour before, and his umbrella was still damp.

He had an appointment with an old friend of his from MI-5. Sir Blair Laggan. "Laggy" had gone into data operations for the government after the war, and then he had used his knowledge to begin a private data collecting and sales concern on an international basis.

It had made him a very, very wealthy man.

Hendricks knew that if one individual could help him bait his trap for Blake Fister and Fister Corporation, it would be Laggy.

And, if Laggy couldn't help him, he would know who could.

Hendricks stopped momentarily on the crowded sidewalks of Baker Street and pretended to use a shop window as a mirror to straighten his tie.

Actually, he was checking to see if he was still being followed.

He was.

A swarthy-looking character with long greasy hair and the soiled clothes of a punk rocker had been following him ever since he'd left his hotel room.

Hendricks knew he couldn't allow himself to be traced to Laggy's corporate data offices. That would immediately tell Fister Corporation—assuming his tail had been sent by Fister—too much about Hayes's and Hawker's plans to topple the company.

As Hendricks reasoned quite coolly, he had two options:

He either had to lose the man who was following him.

Or he would have to kill him.

Hendricks—Sir Halton Collier Hendricks—hadn't killed a human being since 1945.

It was the same year he was awarded his knighthood at Buckingham Palace in a secret ceremony held especially to acknowledge the contributions of British Military Intelligence.

Hendricks remembered his last victim and the circumstances of 1945 very well.

It was May 3, a cool German spring day, in Berlin. It was the day after the Soviets had fought their way into the Nazi capital, and Hendricks was there in his undercover role as a MI-5 agent doubling for the KGB.

Because of his role, he was the first British subject to view the ruin of the Reich Chancellery.

There were bodies everywhere. Bodies on the streets. Bodies piled on wagons. Most were fresh bodies, recently executed by the "liberating" Soviets.

Many of the bodies were those of women. They had been raped, of course, before they were killed. There were more than 90,000 recorded rapes of Berlin women in those last few days of the war.

But Hendricks had no interest in these horrors. Neither did his "tour guide" who, as Hendricks well knew, was another KGB agent sent to accompany him and keep an eye on his activities.

The tour guide's name was Karnakov, and he was a particularly unsavory Russian with bad skin and garlic breath.

Hendricks was there to find Fuehrerbunker—the labyrinth of offices and living quarters built thirty meters underground where Adolf Hitler had directed his broken German war machine during the last 105 days.

Karnakov was there to make sure that, if he did find the secret bunker, all surviving papers and artifacts were to go to Moscow, not London.

Something caught Hendricks's attention as they walked through the bombed-out Chancellery garden. Russians digging. Digging a trench not to bury bodies, but to exhume bodies. Hendricks walked over to observe, and Karnakov tagged along.

There were two bodies, barely distinguishable as a male and a female. They had been badly burned. Oddly, the female corpse was frozen into a sitting position, hands thrown outward as if holding reins. On the belly of the male corpse had been placed the German Iron Cross.

As Hendricks immediately noticed, the medal had not been burned with the bodies. It had been placed there later—probably just before burial.

"Who are they?" Karnakov had asked one of the workers in Russian.

"I do not know," a worker replied, leaning on his shovel, his nose turned away from the stench. "German brass, I guess. All I know is, we have orders to dig in everything around that looks like a fresh grave."

Hendricks didn't have to ask who they were.

He knew.

The Iron Cross had told him.

The charred corpses were those of Eva Braun and Adolf Hitler.

Nonchalantly Hendricks had walked over and taken the Iron Cross from the chest of the corpse. He held it up for Karnakov's inspection, then wrapped it in a handkerchief and put it in his pocket.

He knew Hitler would not have been buried far from his Fuehrerbunker. And, within five minutes, he had found the secret entranceway. With Karnakov right behind him, he had descended the forty-five steps into the dark maze.

For nearly an hour, the two of them did not speak as they went from room to room. In what was obviously Hitler's quarters, Karnakov had paused at a blue horsehair couch. Noticing the bloodstains on it and the floor, Karnakov had wondered out loud if the rumor was true. Maybe Hitler really was dead. Maybe he had committed suicide.

Hendricks had said nothing. Britain's MI-5 was quite sure that Hitler had killed himself. Now there was no doubt in his mind.

But Hendricks hadn't been sent after data on the death of Adolf Hitler. He had been sent after records of communication between the German Abwehr and their spies in England.

MI-5 had convincing evidence that one German agent still roamed London—an agent code-named "Druid."

In the communications shack, the Germans hadn't taken the time to destroy their files. And why should they? The war was obviously lost. With Karnakov looking over his shoulder, Hendricks found a sheath of papers in which the Druid was named several times.

He folded the papers and stuck these, too, in his jacket.

The Russian agent had eyed him suspiciously. "I assume you are taking those back to Moscow?" he asked in bad English.

"London," Hendricks had replied, smiling softly. "I'm afraid I find Moscow rather a dull place. Worse, I find you Russians a barbarous and uncivilized people. If you like, you may consider this my resignation from the KGB."

The insult registered slowly with the KGB agent. As he reached beneath his coat and fumbled to draw his revolver, Hendricks drove the six-inch stainless-steel needle he had been hiding in his hand deep into the Russian's ear.

Karnakov seemed to freeze for a moment. Then he collapsed on the floor, leaking a slight trickle of blood from his head.

Hendricks had walked calmly and coolly up the steps outside.

He smiled pleasantly at the men now wrestling with Hitler's corpse.

He got into Karnakov's jeep and began driving north. He did not stop until American troops with the Third Army flagged him down and asked in their quaint assault on the King's language if there was someplace they could find "Drinking liquor in this god-damn Kraut country worth a shit—and not none of that schnapps crap that tastes like peppermint candy. . . .

That night, Hendricks had billeted at General George S. Patton's headquarters.

After a dinner laid by servants, and over Kentucky bourbon, Hendricks gave an edited report of what he had done and seen that day.

Patton listened wide-eyed, then smacked a big fist on the table and offered him a thousand dollars U.S., guaranteed box seats to the next World Series, and a very ugly white dog in exchange for Hitler's Iron Cross.

After politely inquiring what, exactly, was a "World Series," Hendricks refused.

It had been many years since Hendricks had killed the Russian agent in the subterranean complex of what had been Adolf Hitler's death chamber.

But sometimes it was necessary to kill. When the cause was good, and there was no other way.

The war had taught him that.

Hendricks tapped his bowler hat down and began walking steadily along Baker Street.

At the old Black Stag Hotel, he nodded at the doorman and went inside. Without hesitating, he crossed the lobby and went out the back exit. Quickly then, he walked one more block toward Westminster, then cut through an alley toward Baker Street.

Halfway down the alley, a hand reached out from behind a stack of boxes and jerked him roughly against the damp brick wall.

Hendricks found himself face to face with the greasy-haired punk rocker who had been following him.

"Tried to give me the bloody dodge, you old fart, didn't you?" the young man said in a heavy Cockney accent. There was a knife in his fist, and he pressed the blade against the old butler's throat.

"There's no need to kill me," Hendricks whispered. "If it's money you're after, then I'll give you money."

The punk rocker had a hoarse, phlegmy laugh. "So you think this a stickup, eh, mate?" he grinned. "Well, old top, you might be right. Be easier for the scum at Scotland Yard to understand, hey! A stickup she will be." He slammed Hendricks against the wall again. "Now give me your money, Sir Halton," he added with contempt. "After that, we'll see if Her Majesty's servants bleed the same color as us poor common folk."

Slowly Hendricks reached into his pocket and found what he had been carrying there ever since he had arrived in London.

The metal was cool in his hand.

It was the same stainless-steel needle he had used to kill Karnakov so many years before. . . .

NINE

New York

With his hands cuffed behind him, James Hawker rode moodily as Detective Lieutenant Scott Callis drove them through the heavy Bronx traffic of 10:30 P.M.

"Damn it, Callis," Hawker said finally. "You're wasting time. My time and your time. You know god-damn well I killed those three guys in self-defense."

Callis looked amused. "Do I? And how in the world could I know that? The legal department made us get rid of our crystal balls."

Hawker looked at him. "You won't drop the sarcasm for even a minute, will you? Okay, I'll tell you how you know it was self-defense. First of all, I stuck around after I did it. I made no feverish attempt to rub out my fingerprints, hide my weapon, and try to escape—and I had plenty of time to do all those things, believe me."

"Psychopathic killers are almost always very cool and calm after they waste someone," Callis countered as he turned right and kicked his unmarked car into passing gear on a rare open straightaway.

"Do I strike you as psychopathic?"

"I never did trust guys with reddish hair. Such terrible tempers, you know."

"I'm not even going to react to that, Callis." Hawker shook his head in frustration. "Do you want to hear the second reason why you know it was self-defense?"

"Absolutely," said Detective Scott Callis. "By all means, tell me."

"Because you're a smart cop, that's how you know. I watched you from the time you pulled up. You made all the right moves, did and said all the right things. You've been around, Callis. You know your job, and you've seen enough crooks and murderers to pick them out of a packed stadium."

Callis smiled. "Flattery. I like that. Tell me more."

"Ha," said Hawker. "That's where the flattery ends. You come on smart, Callis, but you end up real dumb."

"Dumb?" The Greek cop raised his eyebrows. "Let me get this straight. I'm free to go wherever I please, and you're sitting there with cuffs on, a murder rap hanging over your head, and you call me dumb?"

Hawker snorted involuntarily. As much as he hated to admit it, he liked Callis. The guy had a weird sense of humor. "How long have you been on the force, Callis?"

As the streetlights flashed by, Hawker saw the look of slyness on Callis's face. "Let's see. . . . Oh, about as long as you were on the Chicago force. Thirteen, fourteen years. Something like that."

Hawker sat up straight. "Just how in the hell did you know I was a Chicago cop?"

Callis began to laugh softly. "About three months ago, at a law enforcement convention in L.A., I ran into a friend of yours.

It took me a while to place your name when you first volunteered it. I knew damn well I had heard that name before. And then I began to match the name with the description. The red-brown hair. That broken beezer of yours. Built like someone had put arms on a stack of bricks—that's the way that funny little Irish detective from the L.A.P.D. described you—"

"Flaherty!" Hawker interrupted.

"That's the guy." Callis chuckled. "I spent the first day there wondering how a mick as dumb as him could ever rise above a uniform corporal. You know—the way he asks those innocuous little questions of his, with that innocent expression and those twinkly blue eyes. Christ, you'd barely give him credit for having enough sense to come in out of the rain. But then one night we were discussing something serious—I forget what—and all of a sudden I realized those innocuous little questions of his were backing me into a corner. Every time I'd change tacks, he'd nail me with another one. Christ, it was like sitting down to a checker game and ending up playing chess against a god-damn grand master! And never once did that twinkly expression of his ever change."

Hawker nodded his understanding and said nothing. That was Flaherty all right.

Hawker had run into the Irish detective when he traveled to California on a freelance mission to help clean up two savage street gangs that were making life hell for the residents in one of the suburbs there.

Flaherty had quickly sniffed out Hawker's careful plans.

He could have sent Hawker to the pen for life.

Instead, Flaherty had stepped back and let him do the important dirty work and then suggested in that sly, wry brogue of his that Hawker might do well to leave L.A. before a certain Irish detective was forced to do his duty.

Hawker didn't need to be told twice.

Flaherty had impressed the hell out of him.

As Callis drove, Hawker shifted uncomfortably in his handcuffs. He wondered how much Flaherty had told Callis. More important, he wondered how Callis had reacted to it. Hawker knew it would be the difference between continuing his work and probably a congressional investigation.

"What got Flaherty talking about me?" Hawker asked carefully.

Callis eyed him shrewdly. "He told me what you did in L.A."

"I did a lot of things in California," Hawker said evasively.

"Yeah, well, I guess you'd remember this. Flaherty said you were a one-man army. Said he'd never seen anything like it. He said you wasted about twenty street-gang members and completely destroyed their organization."

"He said that, did he?" said Hawker. "Jeeze, the guy really has an imagination."

"I don't think imagination has anything to do with it," Callis countered. "Flaherty told me not to be surprised if you turned up in New York one day. That little spud-face said he had 'deduced' that you had some big money behind you and one hell of a lot of motivation."

"Is that all he said?"

Callis dropped every pretense in his voice. "No. He also said that he trusted you and he trusted your judgment. He said that, if I was smart, I'd help you if I ever got the opportunity."

Hawker relaxed a little bit. "And that's why you charged me with murder one?"

"That's right. The way you needled O'Connor and Davis really put you on their shit list. They would have been suspicious if I hadn't gotten tough with you." Callis's dark eyes turned to stone. "I'm always tough on crooks and murderers, Hawker. They know that—and I want you to know that. But, as much as I've sometimes wanted to, I've never had the balls to take it as far as you have."

They had been driving for a long time now. Driving east. As they crossed a high bridge, Hawker suddenly realized they were crossing out of The Bronx.

"Your precinct house is clear over in Manhattan?" he asked.

Callis shook his head. "There's only one reason you would be on Rhinestrauss Avenue, Hawk," he said. "Some way—I don't even want to know how—you heard about Fister Corporation's scam to drive out those old German immigrants."

"Yeah? So if you already know about it, why aren't you doing something about it?"

"Don't play coy, Hawker. You know what it's like. We need hard evidence and court orders and legal wiretaps before we can make a move. That takes time and manpower and money—things we don't have at Pelham Station."

"So what's that have to do with Manhattan?"

Callis's lips drew tight. "Fister Corporation keeps a goon squad on retainer. Renegade Mafiosos. They've got their headquarters over here near the waterfront. They're the ones who have been hitting the folks on Rhinestrauss—and probably the ones in the Lincoln who tried to hit you tonight." Callis looked at Hawker meaningfully. "It's where you might decide to go to work first."

"Does this mean I'm not under arrest?" Hawker said with a dry smile.

Callis fumbled in his coat pocket for something. "It means I want you to tell me what happened tonight. I'll help you get rid of any little flaws in your story. After that, I'll take you back to the precinct for questioning. By then your story should hold water. There will be no apparent grounds for arrest, and I'll be able to release you within an hour on your own recognizance, pending an investigation."

"And what will the investigation find?"

Callis reached over and unlocked Hawker's handcuffs. "I hope it finds that a person or persons unknown have blown Fister Corporation and their fucking goons right out of the water."

TEN

Grand Cayman Island

In the two days before Jacob Montgomery Hayes was kidnapped, he compiled a folder on Fister Corporation potent enough to bring the company to its knees.

He had gathered his information illegally, of course. Hayes had called in debts from old friends, had a half-dozen secret meetings with his bank officers, and put well-placed pressure on banks he did not control to get exactly what he wanted.

And what he found was more disturbing than even he expected.

Blake Fister was more than just an unscrupulous businessman. He was a would-be tyrant on an international level. Fister's dealings in The Bronx were on a very small scale compared to his operations in France, South America, Great Britain, Canada, and West Germany.

And always, his *modus operandi* was the same. He would sniff out businesses or real estate holdings in a vulnerable position, then use strong-arm tactics to buy as cheaply as possible.

His instincts for such situations seemed to be infallible—and that was the most disturbing thing of all. Every large corporation has its own network of spies and intelligence people. A corporation has to to survive.

But Blake Fister's people seemed to be the very best the world's criminal underground had to offer. And even more unsettling than that, Fister had begun moving big chunks of his money into political causes, backing government officials in every country in which he had holdings.

Fister, it seemed, wanted more than just the power of wealth.

He wanted the power of controlling nations.

Jacob Montgomery Hayes was now more determined than ever to stop Blake Fister. But it wouldn't be easy. In the last ten years, Fister had become a recluse, a recluse to a degree that made the late Howard Hughes seem like a publicity hound.

No one knew where he lived. No one knew where or how he worked.

But he *did* work. And he controlled with an iron fist.

It was for that very reason that Hayes knew he must stop him. The world didn't need any more Hitlers.

It had been a busy forty-eight hours, and Hayes was tired. After his second and most productive day on the island, he had driven east out of Georgetown in the battered old Ford he kept there.

The folder he had compiled on Fister Corporation was beside him on the seat.

As he turned down Walker's Road, headed for the thatch-and-wattle cottage he owned at South Sound, a strange feeling of dread came over him. It was the same premonition of death he had experienced the day his young son, Jake, had been murdered—the murder that had brought Hayes and Hawker together in an alliance.

Hayes was too much of a scientist to be superstitious. But he had also studied Zen in Nepal, and he knew the awesome power of the mind.

He didn't live by intuition, but he respected it.

Now his inner mind was trying to tell him something, and Hayes decided to listen.

He pulled over to the side of the road and rummaged through his glove box until he found stamps. He wrote a note on the outside of the Fister Corporation folder, then sealed it in a large brown envelope. He addressed the envelope to a trusted member of his corporate headquarters in Chicago and directed her to Xerox the contents and see that Hawker and Hendricks got copies.

That done, he found a drop box and mailed it before continuing on to his little seaside vacation house.

His house was set back on a long coral drive behind palms and Australian pines. It had been freshly whitewashed, and a path of coquina rock led down to the sea where clear water broke over the reef.

Hayes went inside and poured himself a glass of cold herb tea and added a dash of coconut water.

Ceiling fans stirred the air as he carried his drink to the bathroom and stripped to take a shower. The last thing he did before he stepped beneath the spray was take off his glasses and set them beside his tea.

Without his glasses, he was nearly blind.

Later, he would wonder if the two men had followed him into the house, or whether they had simply waited for him there.

As he soaped his chest, the shower curtain was suddenly thrown back. Hayes looked up to see a blur of dark figures.

"What in the hell do you want!" he demanded.

"You know what we want," said one of the figures in a heavy voice. "You've been collecting some information on a friend of ours. We want it. Now."

Having recovered from his initial shock, Hayes's face became a placid, unreadable pool. "I won't give it to you," he said simply. "And anything you may do to try and get it will be fruitless."

"Oh, yeah?" snarled one of the dark figures. "But you won't be offended if we try, will you?"

Hayes's vision was too bad for him even to see the hand coming.

The figure hit him a stinging slap in the face and, as Hayes brought his hands up to protect himself, hit him again with a heavy fist, full in the scrotum.

Hayes dropped to his knees in the tub.

Barely able to breathe for the pain, he vomited into the drain.

As he vomited, one of the men kicked him in the buttocks, and Hayes lunged face first into the mess.

Just before he passed out, he thought, I can understand Fister's wanting the data. But this sort of cruelty is mindless. It cannot go unpunished. . . .

ELEVEN

New York

Two days after James Hawker was questioned and released, he readied himself for his formal declaration of war on Fister Corporation and the mysterious Blake Fister.

At a Boston Road used car lot, he paid cash for a black Chevrolet van. When the salesman asked him for identification so he could transfer the registration, Hawker slid a hundred-dollar bill onto the table.

The bill disappeared into the salesman's pocket. The salesman looked up and smiled. "Didn't you say your name was John Smith?"

Hawker nodded. "Right."

"Any particular address, Mr. Smith?"

"I'll let you choose one. You know the area better than I do."

Hawker drove the van to the warehouse where Hayes had sent his equipment. He loaded three crates into the van and, once again, paid cash. After lunch at a corner deli, he drove down Rhinestrauss Avenue, past winos sleeping in the smoggy June heat, past the strange bag ladies with their shopping carts full of junk, past an old blind beggar lady with a white cane and a cup full of pencils.

The traffic on the sidewalks was heavier than traffic on the street.

He parked the van outside the two-story brownstone. It rented as separate apartments, and Hawker had leased the upstairs.

He had decided to stay in the German section because he wanted to see if there was a possibility of organizing the neighborhood into a unified body of resistance.

It was always easier to help people when they had the will to help themselves.

As Hawker began to unload the van, the blind lady shuffled past, tapping her cane. As she neared him, she stopped and her head swiveled back and forth as if she sensed the presence of another human being. The woman had stringy gray hair, and she wore an old beret and heavy black glasses.

"*Guten Abend,*" she called out in a shaky voice. "*Guten Aben, lieber Freund!*"

Hawker smiled. "I'm sorry," he said. "I don't speak German."

The old woman tottered around and smiled at him through bad teeth. "But I speak Amerikaner, yes? Quite good, I speak. *Welch schreckliches heiss Wetter!* Oh, what terrible hot weather, no?"

Hawker fished a ten-dollar bill out of his pocket and put it into her can. "The weather is hot, yes." When the old woman made no effort to leave, Hawker added, "Do you live around here?"

The woman nodded emotionally. "*Ja!* Such a nice neighborhood. Now so bad. The men come, buy my house. My husband,

Fritz, such a good man, dead. The men say I must sell our house, so I sell. In Germany, I learn not to argue with the men, *ja!* I sell!"

From the look on her face, Hawker thought she was about to cry. Instead, she steadied herself and she flashed the bad grin again. "You live here, now? *Ja?* I come back some day. Bring you cookies I make. So nice to talk with my *lieber Freunden.* But I must leave soon. The men with guns say, and I do not argue with the men!"

"Come back anytime," Hawker said, lifting one of the crates. "I'll watch for you. And, if things work out, maybe you won't have to leave your home after all."

The woman beamed at him through her dark glasses, then tottered away down the sidewalk.

Hawker watched her until she disappeared around the corner, then carried his load inside.

There was something strange about the woman. Something strange and lonely and pathetic.

New York City, Hawker decided, was the perfect place for her.

At first dusk, Hawker began to ready himself for the fight.

He ate a light supper of fruit and iced tea.

He steamed himself clean in the shower, then forced himself not to flinch as he turned the cold water on full.

He urinated and defecated—two things he didn't want to have to think about in the middle of a firefight.

It was the same well-loved routine he had observed before a baseball game when he played for the Detroit organization, or before a boxing match, back when he was still a teenager, fighting Golden Gloves.

The only difference was, now the stakes were higher.

One hell of a lot higher.

He could feel the butterflies of tension building in his stomach: a good feeling.

Hawker pulled on a black T-shirt and dark jeans. To his ankle, beneath the jeans, he strapped a Randall Attack-Survival combat knife. His best holster—the Jensen Quick-Draw—had been built especially for the customized Colt Commander.

But he no longer owned the Colt.

Lieutenant Callis had insisted that Hawker could not claim the weapon, explaining, "If you say it's yours, I'll have to arrest you all over again. This state's got tough gun laws, and your permit is only good for Illinois."

It was true, so Hawker had not argued.

So, in place of the Colt, Hawker selected the Browning HP 35 pistol. Along with a pretty fair range of effectiveness—seventy meters—the Browning's most attractive feature was its thirteen-round detachable clip. Carefully Hawker filled two clips full of 9mm cartridges and slid a third into the parabellum before housing the pistol in the shoulder holster he had strapped on.

The Browning was dependable, but Hawker had a more effective weapon in mind for the main assault.

From the crate he lifted one of three Ingram MAC10 submachine guns. It was only about twice as long as the Browning and weighed only two kilograms more.

But the Ingram offered one hell of a lot more fire power. The box clip held thirty-two 9mm rounds—and all could be fired, if need be, in just a deadly few seconds.

Hawker loaded five full clips and put them with the Ingram—

along with the Ingram's threaded silencer and a silencer for the Browning—in a canvas knapsack.

Finally Hawker chose the weapon he would use for the initial assault. He had used it before—in L.A.—and he had come to respect it for its silence and its killing power.

It was a Cobra military crossbow. It was small and light, built of aluminum and fiberglass. By breaking it down like a pellet rifle, the weapon cocked itself automatically. It had an effective killing range of more than three-hundred yards, and the deadly, three-edged arrows traveled a hundred meters in less than a second.

Hawker packed a dozen of the small killing bolts, then, using the same professional care, he deposited a few more surprises for the Mafioso goons in the knapsack before locking the rest of his gear away.

That done, he pulled a jacket on over the shoulder holster and tugged a black British watch cap over his red-brown hair. After making sure the cheap lock had sealed the door as best it could, Hawker drew out a six-foot length of piano wire. He would have liked to put it at neck level, but that was impossible because the stair railing was too low. Instead, he strung it tight between two posts at ankle level.

He didn't want any surprises waiting for him when he returned home.

Hawker stepped over the wire and trotted the rest of the way down the stairs. Unexpectedly, the door of the bottom apartment opened. A wedge of light spilled out onto the tiny grass yard, and a figure peered out.

"Hello?" said a woman's voice. "Mr. Hawker? Is that you?"

Hawker stopped and walked toward the figure. It was hard

to make out her features because she was back-lighted. He could only see that she was tall and lithe with fine, straight blond hair cut Dutch-boy fashion. She stood half in the entranceway, holding the door.

"That's right, I'm Hawker," he said, stopping on the sidewalk. "Do we know each other?"

The woman seemed uneasy and just a little embarrassed. "No. My name is Brigitte Mildemar." When Hawker did not immediately respond to that, she added, "I'm the owner of this house."

Hawker nodded and smiled. "Oh . . . *right*. Yeah, I wondered why your name sounded so familiar."

It was a lie. Hawker had leased the flat through a realtor. He had paid no attention to who owned it.

She moved backward into the house a bit—but not enough so that Hawker misread it as an invitation to come in. Even so, he could see her better now. And Brigitte Mildemar was a treat to see. Her hair was white-blond, like spun glass, and it framed one of those sensuous Germanic faces with its high cheekbones, pale-blue eyes that seemed to peer out from caves, and soft chin that curved gently upward toward sunken cheeks.

She was tall—almost as tall as Hawker, who was an inch over six feet. She wore expensive white slacks, pleated and pressed, and a white satin blouse that was primly buttoned at the neck. Even so, it revealed the sharp thrust of small, firm breasts and the narrow veeing of her waist.

She seemed to feel Hawker's eyes on her, and she fidgeted uncomfortably.

"Well," she said quickly, "I heard you coming down the stairs, and I thought I should introduce myself."

"I'm very glad you did . . . Mrs. Mildemar?"

Hawker expected her to blush. She didn't. Instead, her manner became frosty. "It's *Ms.* Mildemar, Mr. Hawker. And now that we have met, I would like to ask you something that I should have perhaps directed my real estate agent to ask—"

"You don't even have to," Hawker interrupted, smiling. "I haven't leased many apartments in my time, but I think I know all the questions. Let's see . . . I don't smoke. I don't drink to excess, and I won't be having any loud parties because I don't like loud parties. Oh, yeah—I don't play any instruments, so you don't have to worry about that. I wish I did, but I don't—unless you count a very bad baritone in the shower. I'm a little bit weak in the pet department, too. No chimps, lion cubs, poodles, or any of the other animals New Yorkers think are so cute and so chic to lead around on a leash." Hawker tapped his finger against his cheek, thinking. "Let's see, anything else? Yes—my hours are irregular." Hawker held up the canvas backpack. "I'm a photographer, you see. I do a lot of night work. Available light stuff, so I'll be coming in late sometimes, but that won't bother you because I am extremely quiet." Hawker gave her a pointed look. "And, of course, any visitors I may invite to my apartment are none of your business."

Some of the coldness left Brigitte Mildemar's eyes as Hawker spoke, replaced by a flicker of amusement. The look of amusement didn't last long.

"That's all very interesting, Mr. Hawker," she countered. "But none of it has anything to do with what I wanted to ask."

"I left something out?"

"Yes. One thing. I'm going to ask you a straightforward question and I want an honest answer."

Hawker smiled. "You're not studying to be the first woman priest or something, are you, Ms. Mildemar?"

Once again, she fought off an amused expression. "No, Mr. Hawker, I am not. What I wanted you to tell me is this: Do you or do you not work for Fister Limited?"

Hawker couldn't help himself. Once he had recovered from his surprise, he burst out laughing.

As he laughed, the woman's face became redder and redder. "Perhaps you will tell me why you find that question so amusing, Mr. Hawker?" she snapped. "For your information, my parents owned this house for a great many years. I grew up here. While I prefer to live in my apartment in Manhattan, I will stay here just as long as I must to make sure the thugs who work for that company don't destroy it in an effort to make me sell." She jammed her hands on her hips. "Now, tell me—why do you find that so funny?"

Hawker wiped his eyes, still chuckling. "Some day, Brigitte, if you ever drop that ice-water facade of yours, maybe I will tell you. Until then, you can rest easy. I don't work for Fister Limited, and I don't work for anyone who's associated with Fister Corporation." Hawker motioned toward his canvas knapsack again. "I'm a photographer, remember? And you know how we artists feel about big corporations."

"Well, then," the woman said primly, "I guess we have nothing more to discuss. It was . . . interesting meeting you, Mr. Hawker."

As she began to push the door closed, Hawker called out, "And, Brigitte—if anyone comes around here from that corporation to bother you again, let me know, okay?"

Hawker thought he saw a dry smile touch the woman's lips before she disappeared inside. "And what would you do, Mr. Hawker?" she answered softly. "Take their photograph and scream for the police? I was raised in New York, and I'm afraid I *do* know how you artists feel—about big corporations . . . and other things."

TWELVE

Fister Corporation's Mafioso goon squad was headquartered in a slummy section of Greenwich Village on the Hudson waterfront in Manhattan.

The lights of the giant tanker moored there couldn't compete with the 11 P.M. skyline of New York. The city was like some humpbacked starship that had put down among the stink and squalor.

But Hawker didn't spend much time gazing at the scenery. His eyes were glued to the three-story warehouse building that Detective Lieutenant Callis had fingered as the Mafioso stronghold.

As Callis had put it, "More bodies have disappeared out those windows into the Hudson River than most undertakers handle in a year. The men you see coming in and out that front door are nothing but scum. Some of them are drug addicts and kill to finance their habit. But most of them just have bugs in their brains. They like to kill. It's how they get their kicks. Hell, the regular Mafia disowned them—that's how sick these dudes are. But they aren't too sick for Fister Corporation. It says something about Blake Fister's methods, doesn't it?"

Callis had paused for a moment, reflecting. He said, "Every now and again, we'll bust two or three of them. But the courts let ninety percent of those we do arrest go free. The other ten percent do three to five years before the parole boards decide they're fit to hit the streets again."

Disgusted, Callis had smacked a big fist into his hand. "I'll tell you, Hawk, just once I'd like to hunt those bastards the way they deserve to be hunted."

So now Hawker was doing just that.

He sat across from the building inside his van. Lights glowed in the windows of the first and second floors.

The third floor was dark.

There seemed to be some kind of meeting going on inside. There was a line of cars parked outside, and Hawker could occasionally see the silhouettes of men crossing before the shades.

He looked at his Seiko Submariner watch. The green numerals said it was 11:14.

Hawker wondered what kind of a meeting it was. Arriving in the middle of a Mafia hoe-down wasn't something he had expected.

As he sat in the van, his brain scanned the various possibilities of what he might do.

The one thing he couldn't do was go through the front door—not without drawing one hell of a lot of attention, anyway. Two stocky guards in cheap suits sat outside the doorway, smoking, expressionless.

It had been Hawker's plan to slip inside, waste anybody who

got in his way, then collar one of the Mafia goons and beat him until he revealed where Blake Fister was and how they communicated with him.

Divide and conquer—that's what he wanted to do. But it wasn't going to be that easy.

Hawker found a stick of chewing gum in his pocket and waited.

He was still waiting at midnight.

Twice he thought the meeting was breaking up when handfuls of men came out and drove off in their cars. But, each time, other cars arrived, and more men filed in—like replacements.

Finally, tired of waiting, Hawker decided he might be missing an ideal chance to get into the building unnoticed. He got his bag of weaponry from the back of the van and stepped out onto the street through the rear doors.

It was a hot, muggy night on the New York waterfront. Out on the Hudson, a tug nudged the silhouette of a massive black barge up the river. Its yellow beacon and green starboard lights added a yuletide note to the white glare of Hoboken. Somewhere, a diesel horn moaned.

Hawker walked calmly down the street, away from the Mafia headquarters. When he was about two blocks away, he cut back across. There was an alleyway beside the building, and he turned down it.

The alley was sour with the stink of garbage and urine. All of the windows of the headquarters had been painted black, so there was no way Hawker could look in. But there was a fire escape—about nine feet above street level.

Hawker slung the knapsack over his shoulder. He jumped

up and grabbed the under-rung of the fire stairs. He was just about to pull himself onto the first step when a voice stopped him cold.

"Freeze it right there, motherfucker! Don't drop. Don't climb. Don't do a god-damn thing—just hang there!"

Hawker saw a huge figure materialize out of the shadows at the end of the alley. The man had a hoarse, gravelly voice that barely exceeded a whisper. He was crouched low, his right fist thrust forward. The stainless-steel revolver he held reflected the weak alleyway light.

The figure came closer. Hawker could make out the wide, meaty bulldog face. The man wore a gray suit, and his hat was cocked jauntily over one eye. A cigarette, freshly lit, smoldered in the corner of his mouth.

Silently Hawker cursed himself for not fixing the silencer onto his Browning before he entered the alley. Even if he did get an opening to use it, the noise would bring the entire goon squad flooding onto the street.

The man with the gun stopped a body length away. Hawker could see his face clearly now. He was grinning. His left eye was wedged shut against the cigarette smoke that curled into it.

"You fucked up bad," the man said as if amused. "You fucked up real bad. No matter why you're here; no matter what you plan to do, 'cause you're dead. You're dead just as sure as I'm standing here."

"Bullshit," Hawker bluffed. "Ask Fister before you go shooting that cap pistol of yours. He sent me. Said something about the feds might be bugging the place. Wanted me to slip in at night and check all the telephone wiring up top."

The man smiled and nodded, but he did not lower his weapon. "So why didn't Fister notify us? You got an answer for that one, smartass?"

"I don't have any answers to anything," Hawker snarled. "And, if I did, I sure as hell wouldn't waste them on you. All I know is what I'm told to do. Now I'm going to drop down—"

"If you do, you're dead," the man snapped.

"How damn long you think I can hang up here?" Hawker demanded, still looking for his opening.

"As long as you want to stay alive—that's how long."

Hawker let go of the fire escape with one hand and swung the canvas bag to the ground. "Look in here if you don't believe me, you dumb shit. All you're going to find is telephone-testing equipment. Hell, I don't even have a penknife on me."

The man looked at the bag suspiciously. "You better not be carrying—because, if you are—"

"Just look in the damn bag," Hawker ordered. "Fister isn't going to like this. He doesn't like one of his administrators taking shit from the hired help."

"Well, I don't know that you *are* with the organization," the man said in mild defense. "But, even if you are, I got my orders, too. I got orders to secure this alley and, by God, that's just what I done."

Hawker was watching him the way a cat watches a bird. His resolve weakening, the man slowly approached the canvas satchel. He took a last look at Hawker before leaning down to inspect it.

The moment he bent over, Hawker jackknifed his legs upward and kicked the man full in the face. The man staggered backward but managed to hang on to his revolver. Hawker came off the fire escape in one fluid motion and used the cutting edge of his right hand to knock the gun to the asphalt.

The Mafia goon swung a wild left that caught Hawker on the side of the head. Hawker stumbled to the ground, his ears ringing. The goon plowed into him, and soon they were a tangle of arms and legs, wrestling for position.

The man was huge—close to three hundred pounds. But Hawker managed to slide around behind him, pulling the Randall survival knife from the scabbard on his calf as he did.

As he did, the goon lurched for his revolver. He rolled and brought the gun up to fire. In the same instant, Hawker drew back the knife and threw it just as hard as he could.

The knife didn't stick.

It didn't need to.

It hit the goon a glancing blow, point first, in the face. Few knives are sharper than the fine Randall, handmade by Bo Randall and his craftsmen in Orlando, Florida. The blade razored the flesh away from his face so that, for the microsecond before the blood began to pour, it looked as if the only thing holding his eye in was the pale cheekbone.

The goon gave a bearish scream, and the gun flew into the air as the man's hands pawed at his ruined face.

Hawker wasn't feeling merciful, but he didn't want to risk the noise of a gunshot. He used his elbow to crack the man unconscious, then retrieved his knife.

The man's scream had drawn enough attention. From the front of the headquarters, Hawker heard a voice inquire, "Hey, Hugo—what's going on in there?"

Hawker returned the knife to its scabbard and slung the knapsack over his shoulder once again. He swung himself up onto the fire escape and trotted silently up the steps to the top floor.

Below him, he could see the two door guards working their way carefully down the mouth of the alleyway.

It would be a matter of minutes before they found the goon, Hugo. And, since the fire escape was the only way out of the alley, Hawker knew he had to buy himself some time.

And the only way to buy time was to stop them.

From the knapsack, Hawker pulled the Cobra crossbow. He cocked the drawstring back and loaded one of the short aluminum killing arrows. He brought the sights to bear on the trailing guard and squeezed his hand closed. There was a thin *whoosh* of air before the man jolted backward, a shocked expression on his face.

He would die with that same expression.

Calmly but quickly, Hawker cocked the bow again and loaded in another killing bolt. The second man swung around as his partner fell.

"Joe—hey, Joe! What the hell's the matter with you?" he demanded. As blood spouted from Joe's chest, it became all too clear what was wrong with him.

The second man swung his gun nervously from one side of the alley to the other, backing away from the fresh corpse.

Hawker brought the Cobra's cross hair to rest on the man's head. He didn't want to give him the chance to fire his weapon reflexively.

The deadly crossbow jolted, and the second man immediately somersaulted backward and landed grotesquely on his knees and neck—with the stub of arrow protruding from his right eye.

Hawker released a long breath of tension before he packed the crossbow away and drew out the Ingram submachine gun. Quickly he screwed the sound arrester into place and switched the weapon to automatic fire.

He headed up the fire escape then, keeping a careful eye on the alleyway below.

He didn't want any more surprises.

The iron steps ended abruptly at a third-floor window. As he expected, the window was locked.

Hawker drew the Randall once again and forced it beneath the windowsill. He moved it back and forth until he found the lock, then smacked the butt of the knife handle until he heard the lock break.

He slid the window open and climbed into the dark room. As he turned to make sure the window didn't slam closed, a voice out of the darkness said, "Drop the weapon, asshole, and press your hands against the wall."

Hawker knew he had used up more than his share of luck, and he didn't believe in second chances.

He didn't drop his weapon and he didn't put his hands against the wall.

Instead, he dove to the floor as three rapid-fire shots crashed through the window above him.

He rolled and came up on one knee, with the Ingram spurting flames. . . .

THIRTEEN

London

When the punk rocker who had been following Hendricks swung him against the brick wall of the alley and reached for the revolver, an inexorable feeling of *déjà vu* came over the old butler.

It was just like the last time, back in Berlin, 1945, when he had killed Karnakov, the Russian.

The moist odor of the alley was similar to the stink of Hitler's bunker. The punk rocker, like Karnakov, was physically repulsive, with bad skin and bloodshot eyes.

Hendricks looked deep into those eyes, just as he had Karnakov's.

And, once again, the stainless-steel needle pick he had used in those last days of the war was still cool to the touch; still cold, innocuous, and lethal.

Hendricks held it now as the punker tightened his grip on the old butler's neck, squeezing until Hendricks thought his windpipe would collapse.

"You've reached the end of the line, *Sir* Halton," the Cockney hood whispered as he lifted the knife. "And rarely has a job given me such pleasure, because, me boyo, I got a real thing about you proper Londoners."

Slowly Hendricks brought the steel needle up as if he were making a helpless gesture to knock the punker's left hand from his throat. But, at the last moment, he used his knees to drive the needle up through the soft underside of the hood's jaw, deep into his cranium.

The punk's eyes grew wide and glassy, still looking into Hendricks's eyes. The knife clunked to the brick pavement as he released his grip on the butler's throat. He took two choppy steps backward as he brought his hand up and searched the underside of his jaw. It was as if he only wanted to straighten the tie he did not wear.

Strangely, he looked at the knife on the ground, then looked at Hendricks. His face showed both surprise and fear.

His mouth opened as if to speak, but only a guttural *aurrggg* passed his lips before he took three more mechanical steps and collapsed in a heap.

Calmly Hendricks checked both ends of the alley to see if anyone had observed.

No one had.

Quickly then, he went to the dead Cockney hood and drew out the needle and wiped it clean on the corpse's slacks.

Before continuing on his way, Hendricks straightened his bowler and slid the needle back into the lining of his pocket.

In the distance, Big Ben gonged out 3 P.M.

Hendricks realized he would have to hurry if he didn't want to be late for his meeting with Laggy.

* * *

Sir Blair Laggan's offices were in the old Brougham Building near Westminster—one of the few major nineteenth-century structures that had escaped Luftwaffe bombs.

Hendricks presented his card to the doorman and, a few moments later, was ushered inside.

The interior of the building was a model of understated English grandeur: coats of arms, red tapestry, suits of armor standing guard over a hundred generations of tradition.

Sir Blair's offices were on the eighth floor. Hendricks rode up on an ornate old lift with a gilded telescoping door. But once he reached the eighth floor, the remnants of England's past peeled away, and Hendricks was deposited into an ultra-modern complex of neon lights, room-sized memory banks, and employees working intently at their computer terminals.

Hendricks removed his bowler in the presence of the young receptionist, a striking redhead with wonderfully long legs and fierce blue eyes.

She looked up from her typewriter and smiled at him. "Sir Halton? Sir Blair says he is very anxious to see you. He's in a meeting right now, but he said I was to take you directly to his office." Her grin widened, and an even stronger Irish brogue crept into her voice as she added, "Sir Blair says you are to receive VIP treatment. Called you by a pet name, he did. 'Hank,' was it?"

Hendricks allowed himself a rare smile. "Quite," he said. "One would expect Laggy to remember such a thing."

The receptionist put her hands to her face, delighted. "Laggy! What a funny thing to call Sir Blair." She stood and came around the desk, her hand outstretched. "My name is Mary Kay—and if I promise not to tell a soul Sir Blair's nickname . . ." She paused for effect. ". . . would you hold me to it?"

"On my honor, I would not," Hendricks said with a laugh.

As the Irish receptionist led him to Sir Blair's office, she pointed out some of the computer equipment by name and number. It meant nothing to Hendricks, but he could see that the woman was anxious to please him, so he pretended to the interested. He didn't have to pretend to be impressed. The entire short tour was accompanied by the plastic clatter of printers and the cool hum of the massive electronic brains.

At Sir Blair's office, Hendricks once again passed through a time warp, from the very new to the old and traditional. His office was spacious and stately, with plush carpet and heavy furniture of brass and mahogany. His huge desk sat in front of a window that showed the London skyline. Across from the desk were chairs, a cherrywood table, and a couch. Nearby was a full bar.

It was there that the receptionist seated him.

"Now," she said, "is there anything I can get you? A whiskey, perhaps? Or a nice cup of tea? Sir Blair has taken the liberty of ordering your dinner, but if you would like anything else—a place to freshen up, or a—"

"I'll have a Scotch," Hendricks interrupted. He was still shaken by his fight with the Cockney, and he felt a drink might steady him. "Heavy glass. A full two fingers. And no ice."

Hendricks spoke like a man who was used to being obeyed, and he was slightly amused at how quickly he had fallen back into his old character: the intelligence officer he had been forty years before.

The Irish receptionist set his drink on the table, and the door *whooshed* closed behind her.

Hendricks nursed his drink. It was nearly half gone before the door opened again and in walked his old friend, Blair Laggan. The two men had not seen each other since a group reunion in the early 1950s but, even so, there was no gushing of emotion as they shook hands and took seats.

"You're looking well, Laggy," Hendricks began. "Put on a stone or two, eh?"

Sir Blair Laggan patted his stomach and chuckled. "This blasted new company chef we have, Hank—as you will soon see. French chap. A bloody artist in the kitchen, what? We'll be taking our meal here. Do you mind? I've ordered chops, cold asparagus, fresh vegetables, broiled potatoes—and a brace of marrow bones." Laggan smiled. "I got to thinking about that time in France when you had such an awful yearning for the bloody things."

"A long time ago, Laggy."

Sir Blair nodded, still patting his stomach. During the war years, he had been steel straight and hard as whipcord. Now, dressed in his gray business suit, Blair Laggan looked like the stereotypical English businessman. His black hair was thinning at the crown, and the plump face peered out upon the world through thick glasses. Now his blue eyes—magnified hugely by the glasses—studied Hendricks. "Ah, but you, Hank. You've hardly changed a bit. Still tall and hard, with that poker face of yours—" Sir Blair stopped in midsentence. "Why, what's happened to your neck, Hank? You've a bruise knot on your throat the size of a golf ball! And your shirt—there's blood on it!"

Hendricks dismissed it with an open-handed gesture and a sheepish look. "Baker Street was a bit slippery after the rain, Laggy. I'm afraid my legs aren't as trustworthy as they once were. Took bit of a fall. Nothing, really."

"But you'll want to see a doctor, old boy. The company keeps one on staff. In house all day long. Poor chap is usually bored stiff, so let me give him a ring, what?"

Hendricks refused and quickly shifted the conversation to other things.

It was the kind of chatter Hendricks normally loathed. To him, old memories were little more than twice-told gossip. Even so, he steered the talk through the war years because he thought it might put Laggan in the proper mood to help.

Sir Blair clearly enjoyed the reminiscence—often using it as a segue to the present. It was obvious that Laggan's people had kept the files of everyone involved with Military Intelligence up to date—including Hendricks's.

"Do you remember Reggie Collins?" Sir Blair asked as he refilled Hendricks's glass. "Yes, of course you do. You worked with him for a time in MI-5? Right. English chap, raised in Mother Russia. Picked him up during the war as KGB and turned him. Quite useful, or so he seemed."

Hendricks nodded. "Yes, I remember Reggie. Worked quite closely on a mission or two."

"Well, Hank, he was arrested about five months ago—maybe you read about it? No? It was quite a scandal. Reggie had a seat in the House and was privy to all sorts of secret reports. After all of these years, of course, the government had confidence in him—but it became evident important information was being leaked from a very high source. Had been for some time. Prime stuff, too. Now it turns out that Reggie hadn't left the KGB at all. Even had ties into the Abwehr years ago." Laggart pushed his glasses back to emphasize his next point. "Even some talk around that he's the bloody Druid—the German spy you could never quite get your hands on."

"The Druid?" said Hendricks in disbelief. His last mission from MI-5 had been to track down the Druid. It was the one mission at which he had failed. "I can't believe that anyone would care anymore," he added. "My God, the Nazis are long gone. Of what possible interest can the Druid be now?"

Sir Blair was about to reply when there was a knock at the door and servants began bringing in their dinner. The two old friends seated themselves at the table and began to eat.

"Of what value is the Druid now?" mused Sir Blair, waving a chop at him. "Well, for one thing, the Druid would possess unique information. Data, Hank, data. Information has become the new international tender. It's more liquid than gold, and sounder than the dollar." Laggan raised an eyebrow. "And I'll tell you something, Hank, old man. Hitler was a prophet in that regard. Had a tremendous respect for data. As you know, there are a great many mysteries about those last days of the war. The Third Reich's emergency fund—all in diamonds and gold. What happened to it? And, it has also been rumored that Hitler and Goebbels left exacting orders—on microfilm—about how their successor should rebuild the German Empire. Goebbels himself said they were planning for the year 2,000—not 1940. And that awful Bormann, Hitler's second—no one really knows what happened to him.

Data, Hank, data. Hitler knew what it would someday mean to the world."

"Quite right." Hendricks smiled. "Corporal Hitler knew and so, obviously, did you, Laggy. You stayed in the business."

"A bit of luck, that," Sir Blair said modestly. "My corporation does basically the same thing we used to do for MI-5, Hank, but now we do it for private enterprise *and* governments. Very little of the old cloak-and-dagger stuff, though. You won't find me down in any bunkers eliminating Russians with ice needles, or liberating any Iron Crosses." Laggan raised his eyebrows comically. "Still, we have our moments. Some of them quite exciting."

Hendricks was silent for a moment, deep in thought. "Yes," he said finally. "I understand." Then, looking up and smiling warmly, Hendricks began without preamble his story about Fister Corporation. He gave him the background information clearly and concisely, omitting only the incidents with the assassin, Renard, and the Cockney punk.

Laggan listened carefully, asking appropriate questions.

When Hendricks had finished, Sir Blair dabbed at the corners of his mouth with a napkin. "And that's all you want me to do, Hank? Build an electronic folder on you that will convince this Blake Fister person you are an international financier?"

"Quite right," said Hendricks. "And, of course, I would also like to find out how to get into his inner circle. If I can gain his confidence as a very wealthy investor, then we can work from the inside out. But I understand he is quite careful about whom he will see."

Laggan shrugged. "I know nothing about the man, but I will have a computer search done on him. I'll have my private secretary, Mary Kay, do it. Wonderful girl, bright as a new penny. Do you remember my old batman, Sergeant Mooney? A wild Irish rebel, that. Mary Kay is his daughter. Does all my private research."

"She's discreet?"

"Absolutely," Laggan said. "I'll have her cross-check all references until, I don't doubt, we will have a very full dossier on him. From that, we should get leads enough to track the fellow down. Contriving a folder on you, Hank, will be no problem at all. We will, of course, have to fix you with a *nom de plume*."

"I don't want to get you into any trouble, Laggy."

Sir Blair tossed his napkin on the table, then removed a long, thin cigar from a polished box. "Nonsense, Hank!" he insisted. "I don't want to blow my own whistle, but really, I've become something of an authority on moving and manipulating information. I've always done it honestly—true. But this one indiscretion should be permitted." He lighted the cigar and exhaled blue smoke. "After all, we worked very hard together during the war."

Hendricks nodded. "We did indeed, Laggy."

Sir Blair Laggan stood and held out his hand. "I only wish I could do more for you, Hank. Nothing's too good for my old friends—that's what I always say. We should have you rough and ready in about . . . twenty-four hours?"

"That soon?"

The Englishman smiled. "Sooner, probably."

Hendricks found his bowler and umbrella, then stopped at the door. "There is one more thing, Laggy. That business about Reggie Collins interests me. I feel a bit silly admitting it, but the

Druid affair has always been a bit of a bee in my bonnet—failed mission and all. Where are they keeping the scoundrel?"

Sir Blair's face showed surprise. "You want to see him?"

Hendricks's manner was off-hand. "Oh, if I get the time and it's not too far."

"Quite a distance, I'm afraid, Hank," Laggan said, puffing his cigar reflectively. "A maximum security prison. The Queen's best. But it's in Ireland. The north of Ireland. Near a little Atlantic village called Loughros Moor."

Hendricks tapped the bowler on his head. "Too bad, then. I guess I'll just have to consider the case closed."

FOURTEEN

New York

When the three shots shattered the window above him, James Hawker came up on one knee and held the Ingram submachine gun on automatic fire, spraying the darkness with 9mm slugs.

A man's scream pierced the chain-rattle thunk of the Ingram's silencer, and—suddenly—there was light.

Clawing at the wall was a man Hawker had never seen before. The man had somehow hit the overhead light switch in his agonized writhing. Blood outlined his handmarks on the wall. A large scarlet bubble had formed on his lips. Three black holes in his chest marked the Ingram's deadly pattern.

The man's dark eyes were empty, staring into Hawker's. The bubble on his lips burst. "You . . ." he said in a strangled voice. "You. . . ."

Hawker calmly stood, ejected the spent clip, and jammed a fresh load into the little submachine gun. He watched the man idly, waiting for him to finish his last sentence.

But the man died with his thought unfinished, the unspoken words lost in the glassy stare of death as he crumpled to the floor.

Hawker nudged the corpse out of the doorway with his foot. He peered out into the dark hall. From the stairwell came the sound of voices. Men's voices:

"Barney—what the hell's going on up there?"

Hawker trotted back to the shattered window and looked out. A half-dozen more men stood in the alley, blocking his escape. They had found the three corpses.

One of the men saw Hawker at the window and snapped off a quick shot. The slug ricocheted off the wall of the building, stinging Hawker's face with shards of brick. Hawker wiped the sting away, feeling the blood warm on his hand.

He didn't give the man a chance to shoot twice.

He brought the Ingram to his hip and sprayed the narrow alley. The man who had shot at him took one step as if to run, but the 9mm slugs cut his legs from beneath him. His hands beat madly on the pavement, and then he went suddenly still.

The other men either turned to run or dove for cover—cover that didn't exist.

None of them made it.

One by one, the Ingram chopped through their bodies. For Hawker, who held the Ingram, it was like touching them with an electric probe. They jerked and jolted, and died with the screams on their lips.

Once again Hawker punched the empty clip free and slid a fresh thirty-two rounds into the smoking weapon.

There could be no running from this fight. He had fought his way in, and now he would damn well have to fight his way out again.

Or die trying.

Lieutenant Scott Callis had said it best. The goons who inhabited this building—men who killed to finance their drug habits, or killed for the sick pleasure of inflicting pain—didn't deserve the benefits of a benevolent judicial system.

They lived like rabid animals, and they should be hunted like such.

Hawker had just declared war on them.

It was a war only one could walk away from.

And Hawker was determined that he would be the only one to walk away.

There was no doubt they had him trapped. But there was one thing he couldn't afford—to be caught in a crossfire. Somehow he had to keep his rear covered."

Hawker quickly dug into his canvas knapsack and produced a sausage-sized roll of C-4, military plastic explosive. He broke off a baseball-size chunk of it and molded it to the shattered window. Then he took a detonator attached to a D-size flashlight battery and a blasting cap. Hawker stuck the blasting cap into the C-4 and ran the wire across the open window.

Anyone who tried to climb through that window would get the surprise of his very, very short life.

Hawker trotted back to the dark hallway.

The voices downstairs were louder now, and there were heavy footsteps echoing in the stairwell. Hawker waited until the first figure appeared at the second-floor junction of the stairs, then cracked off three careful shots with the Ingram. A short, fat man screamed and grabbed his chest as his stub-nosed revolver was catapulted into the wall behind him. The man grabbed the handrail, then tumbled over it. He landed with a sickening thud on the bottom floor.

From below, an enraged voice yelled out, "We don't know who you are, motherfucker, but you're dead. You got that! You . . . are . . . *dead!*"

Hawker couldn't resist. "Talk's cheap," he taunted with a laugh.

When he was sure they weren't going to try another charge up the stairs, Hawker moved down the hallway to the other side of the building. As he suspected, there was another fire-escape ladder there. The moment he pressed his face against the window to get a look into the second alley, the Mafia goons below opened fire.

Hawker got his head back just in time.

From his knapsack, he took out a pint container of Astrolite, the liquid military mine explosive. Hawker had used it before. It was easy to carry, easier to use, and, best of all, it could only be detected by specially trained military dogs.

Hawker doubted if this band of Mafia killers had access to such a dog.

Hawker squirted the entire pint in the hall between the stairs and the second fire escape.

If he didn't have to use it, it would lose its effectiveness after four days and be completely harmless.

But Hawker hoped they gave him reason to use it.

He returned to the window of the second fire escape and drew more fire but purposely did not return it.

When he heard the first sound of someone pulling himself up onto the ladder, he ducked back down the hall and stopped at the stairwell.

"Hey, down there," he yelled. "I'm ready to negotiate. You hear me?"

"Yeah, we hear you, asshole," a gravelly voice called back. "And as far as I'm concerned, you got nothing to negotiate except how you die."

Hawker tried to give his voice just the right touch of desperation. "You got no reason to kill me, buddy. Here's what I'll do. I'll tell you who sent me—in exchange for my life. That's fair, isn't it? Look, I've got enough hardware up here to blow you bastards to kingdom come. But there's no sense—"

"You're bluffing, asshole!" retorted the voice. "You're just about out of ammo, aren't you? And now you're whining for your life. It ain't gonna wash, dumb fuck. We're coming up there, and when we get done, you're going to beg us to kill you."

Sure now that the trap had been set, Hawker retreated to a room at the rear of the building. He switched on the overhead light and forced the window. The window opened into a dead-air space between the Mafia headquarters and the building behind it.

Hawker had hoped to find a ledge there, but there was none. He was about to return to the stairs and fight it out, when he noticed an attic door set into the ceiling. He climbed up on a chair and pushed the door back. It opened into a space between the third floor and the roof.

Hawker crawled through the dust and stink toward a rectangle of light at the far edge of the attic. It was a wooden vent. Hawker kicked the vent away and stuck his head out to see the blackness of the Hudson River, three stories below. A pair of roosting pigeons fluttered wildly into the city darkness as he pushed himself through, onto the roof.

The roof of the building stunk of asphalt and bird guano, and it was still hot from the summer sun.

Hawker got to his feet and was just about to check on the progress of the men at the second fire escape when a sudden explosion shook the whole building, throwing chunks of the roof high into the city sky.

Hawker dropped to his belly and covered his head as debris tumbled down.

For a wild moment, he thought he had accidentally hit the electronic detonator in his knapsack and set off the Astrolite.

But then he remembered the booby-trap he had planted at the first window.

Hawker got shakily to his feet, making a mental note to use less C-4 plastic explosive next time.

If he lived to see a next time.

Hawker walked to the new crater in the roof and stared down into the room where he had first entered the building. The entire wall was gone, and most of the floor, so he could see right through to the second story. There were still only three corpses in the alley. Whoever had set off the booby-trap had been scattered in pieces with the debris.

Moving quickly, Hawker crossed the roof to the other side of the building. Four Mafia goons had worked their way up the second fire escape in single file. Hawker could have wasted all of them, but he didn't want to give away his position.

If the hunter moves too quickly from the blind, he will frighten the tiger.

And Hawker didn't want to lose this tiger. Not now. He had a feeling they wouldn't make it so easy for him next time.

He still had one major obstacle to overcome. He had to get back down to the ground floor.

If he waited for the four men on the fire escape to go inside, there was a chance he could work his way down the brick facade of the building to the iron ladder. But that was damn risky.

His second option was to try to jump from the Mafia headquarters to the next building, then hope to find a skylight entrance or another fire escape.

The third option was, at best, an emergency exit—to plunge the forty feet into the black Hudson River and hope that the water was deep enough and there were no submerged pilings to hit.

Hawker considered the water below. If the fall didn't kill him, the pollution might.

Hawker opted to jump to the next building.

The dead-air space between the Mafia headquarters and the broken-down apartment behind it was about twelve feet. That wasn't much in a broad jump pit, but it looked a hell of a lot farther at night. Three stories high. With nothing to break his fall but the asphalt below.

After pacing off the distance, Hawker got a running start—and hit a slick spot and skidded just as he pushed off with his left leg. For a long, sickening microsecond, Hawker knew that he wasn't going to make it. He flapped wildly in midair like a dying bird. All he could think of was that, if the fall didn't kill him, the Mafia thugs would take their own sweet time about finishing him off.

It was that thought which probably gave Hawker the will to stretch out the extra inch or so it took to lock his fingers on the lip of the next roof. His left hand slipped off at impact, but his right hand held firm, fingers digging, arm muscle straining, legs frozen perfectly still so as not to throw off his tenuous balance.

Slowly then, Hawker got his left hand back on the roof and held there for a moment, trying to regain his composure.

Below he heard footsteps and loud voices. If they saw him now, he was dead.

But that was a secondary worry.

Right now, he had to concentrate on pulling himself up onto the safety of the roof.

FIFTEEN

Grand Cayman

Jacob Montgomery Hayes awoke, expecting sunlight to stream through the window with the sound of morning birds.

It was, after all, a bad dream.

Or was it?

As his eyes adjusted to the tropical darkness, his brain began to locate the injuries his body had suffered and began to register the intensity of the pain. It left him with the stark truth:

This was no dream.

If anything, it was hell.

Painfully, Hayes turned his head and looked at the glowing numerals of the desk clock. It was the one bit of hard reality they had allowed him. A clock. Something with which to measure the suffering.

It was 1:13 A.M.

Hayes tensed as he saw the time. They would be coming soon. Every four hours without fail, they came. They came with their lengths of surgical tubing and their rubber gloves, and their scalpels.

Always the questions were the same: What had he done with the folder on Fister Corporation? Who else knew? Who was helping him?

Hayes allowed his head to fall back on the table where he was strapped, hands and legs, nude. An examination table—the kind you see in doctors' offices.

But these men were not doctors.

Quite the opposite.

They were killers. They were ghouls who enjoyed inflicting pain. Professionals who knew how to inflict pain without damaging the body.

But, so far, Hayes had bested them. So far he had refused to speak a word. Every time they came with their instruments of pain, he would draw on his Zen training—the ability to rise out of his own body and block out all earthly suffering; the power of *zazen* he had learned so many years before at the monastery on Crystal Mountain in the thin air of the Himalayas.

Again and again the words of his beloved Roshi returned to him:

"*When your concentration becomes strong, instead of hobbling you, pain will spur you on if you use it bravely. . . .*"

Now Hayes was using his pain as bravely as he could. He had no thoughts for his own life. He had lived his life fully, and, besides, it was the nature of Zen to understand that one's own life means nothing.

But he had to hold out to give his friends Hawker and Hendricks time. Time to close in on the man who called himself Blake Fister. Time to learn his awful secret, and to destroy him.

Slowly the minutes slid by. Hayes could hear the crash of the

Caribbean surf outside. He could smell the sweet scent of citrus and frangipani.

Twenty-four minutes after one by the clock on the desk.

Hayes wondered what Hawker was doing right now. Alive, certainly—for no one knew better how to stay alive than James Hawker.

Asleep, perhaps. Yes, James would certainly be asleep.

There was noise in the hallway, and the lights flashed on. Hayes's eyes rebelled against the glare of the neon.

Three men came into the room. Two of the men were in their late thirties or early forties. They were the men who had kidnapped him.

The third man was a Napoleon-sized man, squat and thick, with jet-black hair greased straight back. Despite his age, his paunchy face and lively dark eyes retained the confidence of youth. He was dressed in a white smock, like a surgeon.

Hayes noted the relish with which he pulled on the rubber gloves and then, idly, toyed with the mole above his left eye before selecting an instrument from the tray beside the table.

"Have you yet decided to speak to us, Mr. Hayes?" the man asked with a thin smile.

Hayes did not answer. He settled back on the table, willing his body to relax.

"No?" the man said, as he threaded one piece of surgical tubing into another. "Well, now, we must convince you then. Your stubbornness is to be admired—but hasn't it gone on long enough?"

Hayes closed his eyes as they used a pair of tongs to hold his penis and forced the tubing up him, probing at his bladder.

At first, their questions echoed loudly through the ripping pain. But then he willed his center of consciousness to drop low and deep within him, letting the words of his Roshi blot out all other feeling:

"One must meditate with a sense of dignity and grandeur, like a mountain or a giant pine, aloof of all worldly things. . . ."

It was one thirty in the morning.

The torture would last until after two.

SIXTEEN

London

From a sound sleep, Hendricks sat bolt upright in bed. His heart was pounding, and he didn't know why.

He listened carefully, staring hard into the darkness. Outside, rain fell against the window in a steady drizzle. There was the distant hiss of traffic in the streets as late travelers hurried through the cavern of London Town.

Hendricks threw back the covers and switched on the table lamp. His pocket watch had been placed neatly on the vanity along with his billfold, a brush, and a lethal-looking Walther PPK.

Hendricks looked at the watch.

Forty minutes after six in the morning.

What in the hell had woken him?

Disturbed by the strange anxiety that now flooded him, Hendricks picked up the cold weight of the automatic and began a methodical search of his room.

He was barefoot and wore gray pajamas.

All the closets were empty, the door to the hallway locked and chained.

Hendricks ran a hand through his close-cropped hair and sat back on the bed. Something was wrong, but what?

His old military atlas was on the desk. Absently he picked it up and began to leaf through it.

Earlier that evening, he had used it to ascertain the location of Loughros Moor, Northern Ireland.

Now he found himself irresistibly drawn to the maps of the Indian subcontinent.

Tibrikot? Ring Mo? Crystal Mountain?

Why should villages in the Himalayas suddenly be of such intense interest?

Hendricks immediately thought of Jacob Hayes. Hayes had studied there—but how could that account for his unreasonable urge to review the atlas?

He placed the Walther back on the desk. He stared at the phone. For some reason, he felt he should try to contact Hayes. It was a strong, almost overpowering urge. But it would be nearly 2 A.M. in Grand Cayman.

Hayes would think he was crazy.

Feeling strange and silly, Hendricks reluctantly climbed back into bed and switched off the lamp.

He had nearly an hour before he had to get up.

And the ferry ship to Dublin rarely left on time anyway.

He decided he would call Hayes before he left for Ireland.

SEVENTEEN

New York

Hanging from the lip of the roof, Hawker did not move until he heard the footsteps pass beneath him.

Then slowly, so he would not lose his grip, he pulled his head above the tarpaper and locked his chin on the gravelly surface before bracing his elbows on the roof and hauling himself safely up.

He rolled several feet away from the precipice, then lay there for a time, breathing deeply.

He didn't fear death from a bullet. But the idea of busting his back in some Greenwich Village shithole didn't appeal to him.

Brushing the gravel off his pants, Hawker stood. The green numerals of his Seiko said it was 1:45 A.M.

Strangely, strong thoughts of Jacob Montgomery Hayes suddenly coursed through his mind. Strong thoughts with strong images: Hayes, dressed in white, sitting beneath a fir tree on a mountain snowpeak.

With the thoughts came a momentary feeling of dread.

If Hawker had been a superstitious man, he might have

wondered if Hayes was trying somehow to communicate with him—that's how vivid the sudden image was.

But Hawker—like Hendricks who, at that very moment, was sitting in a London hotel room studying a map of the Himalayas—wasn't a superstitious man.

And, besides, he didn't have time to think about it right now.

After making sure none of his weaponry had spilled out in his near-fall, Hawker moved on across the roof. He was looking for another fire escape so he could get back down to street level.

The building had a fire escape—but it ended abruptly at the second floor. Cursing beneath his breath, Hawker realized he was going to have to jump to yet another building.

The next building in line was in better shape. There were lights in the windows. People probably kept offices there—though it now appeared empty.

But, more important, its fire escape was in proper condition. Hawker could see it plainly in the dim light.

He backed up, took a deep breath, got a good run, and jumped.

This time, he made it without incident.

Quickly he climbed down the iron steps to the street. If anyone had heard the shooting in the Mafia headquarters, there was no sign of it. Hawker had the feeling that, if vigilante hangings were held in downtown New York, no one would make the effort to look—let alone try to stop them.

Hawker walked through the darkness of the alley and peered out onto the street.

All three floors of the Mafia headquarters were lighted now. He could see men crossing before the second-floor windows.

They had made it that high. Soon they'd gather their courage and head to the third floor—and that's when he would hit them.

Hawker trotted down the street, wary of being spotted.

The front door of the headquarters was open. There were no guards to be seen.

Hawker ducked beneath the two front windows, then swung into the doorway, the Ingram at his hip, freshly loaded and ready.

It was a broad room with bare wooden floors and long tables. There were rows of liquor bottles on the counter, and the whole place stank of cigarette smoke and sweat.

Except for the occasional shuffle of footsteps upstairs, the building was deathly quiet. Hawker guessed they must have regrouped and were moving as a team now.

He wondered how many there were.

If they made it to the third floor, it didn't matter.

Quietly he crossed the room to the stairwell. The corpse of the short, stocky man he had killed still lay on the floor where he had fallen. The man's eyes were wide and glassy, and a fecal stink oozed from the pool of blood beneath him.

Hawker stepped over the dead man and looked up the stairs. At that moment, a voice from the second floor called out, "Hey—asshole! You listening?"

For a shaky moment, Hawker thought they had spotted him. But then he realized they were trying to get him to answer from the third floor—probably to pinpoint his exact location.

Hawker said nothing.

"Look," the voice continued, "maybe we can work out some kind of deal or something. Hey—you hear me?"

Slowly Hawker began to work his way up the stairs, the little submachine gun, with its tubular silencer, vectoring ahead of him.

Three quarters of the way up the stairs, just when Hawker thought he had it made, just when he began to grow confident he could take them by surprise, there was a stumbling, grunting noise behind him. Hawker whirled around to see a man with a revolver sprawled belly-first on the floor at the base of the stairs.

He had seen Hawker apparently and was sneaking in for the kill when he somehow tripped—probably over the corpse.

The dead man would never know it, but he had saved Hawker's life.

The man who had tripped brought the revolver quickly up to fire.

Too quickly.

The shot shattered plaster behind Hawker's head. Hawker squeezed off two careful shots, and the man's face disintegrated into a pulpy mess.

Hawker didn't have much time to enjoy the irony of it.

Footsteps pounded the floor above him, and two men swung into view at the top of the stairs. Their handguns roared in the narrow confines of the stairwell.

Hawker dropped low on the steps, hugging the wall. He had a narrow view of their heads, but it was enough.

He held the submachine gun on automatic fire, and the two faces exploded open, then disappeared like clay targets at a shooting gallery.

He could hear more voices behind him now. He swore softly under his breath.

This is exactly what he had most desperately wanted to avoid. Getting caught in a crossfire.

He had one chance, and one chance only.

He had to drive the men on the second floor to the third floor, then turn immediately and fight his way back outside.

Hawker drew the Browning automatic from beneath his jacket with his left hand and peppered the front doorway with four quick shots as the first man tried to come through.

The man screamed and spun away, holding his stomach.

Hawker punched the near-empty clip from the Ingram and slid in the last fresh clip he had.

There were still nine rounds left in the Browning, and he had thirty-two in the submachine gun.

It would have to be enough.

Hawker took a deep breath and, with a weapon in each hand, he charged up the stairs, taking the steps two at a time.

There were at least seven men at the top of the stairs—probably more. The last thing they expected was for Hawker to attack. He could read the shock plainly in their faces.

He held the trigger of the Ingram down, clearing the path ahead, while squeezing off a steady stream of fire from the automatic pistol.

Two of the men jolted backward, clawing at their ruined faces. The others bolted up to the building's next level to join their remaining comrades.

It was exactly what Hawker had hoped they would do.

The Browning was empty, but there was no time to reload

now. Hawker jammed it back into his shoulder holster and drew out the Randall Attack-Survival knife.

If someone jumped him from behind, he wouldn't have the opportunity to fight him off with his fists.

And there was no way they were going to take him alive.

EIGHTEEN

With both weapons ready, Hawker ran back down the stairs. At the door, he paused and peered outside. One of the Mafia goons swung around the corner, and Hawker used the Ingram to chop him down.

Hawker knelt in the doorway.

He wasn't in the safest place to touch off the Astrolite, but he had no choice.

If he took the time to fight his way down the street—assuming there was opposition—the others would wise up and follow him out.

Waiting only long enough to make sure no one had followed him down the stairs, Hawker slid the knapsack off his shoulder and found the electronic detonator. He flipped up the safety lid and paused before hitting the transmitter button.

"Have a nice flight, boys," he said out loud as he pressed the red square.

The device hummed . . . was momentarily silent . . . then a deafening roar shook the entire building.

The force of the explosion knocked Hawker to the ground. Plaster rained down on him followed by a massive ball of heat and smoke that came tumbling across the room from the stair-well.

Hawker expected to hear screams of pain and calls for help.

But there were none.

There was only a strange and eerie silence as the last of the debris clattered to the earth.

The Astrolite had done its job well.

Hawker got quickly to his feet and brushed himself off.

He had to hurry now.

New Yorkers might be able to ignore gunshots, but no one could ignore an explosion of that magnitude. Even though the waterfront was comprised mostly of old and deserted industrial buildings, someone somewhere had to be calling the police at that very moment—if they hadn't been called already.

Hawker stepped out onto the sidewalk, surveying the street.

It was oddly deserted and quiet. There wasn't much time for conservative movement now. Hawker took one more look down the street, then set out toward his van at a weary trot.

"Freeze, asshole!"

The voice came from behind him and to his right. In mid-stride, Hawker turned and dropped to his belly on the pavement, and waved the Ingram in the general direction of the voice.

The submachine gun sputtered twice, then was silent.

It was empty.

Hawker could see the figure coming at him: a short, thin man wearing the kind of hat you see in old gangster movies.

A lance of orange flame jumped from his hand, and the asphalt exploded just to the left of Hawker. Hawker rolled as still another slug smacked into the street beside him.

Hawker realized with a cold resolve that he had no chance against the man.

He was dead, would be dead within a matter of seconds . . . unless he could somehow throw the Randall knife with enough force to knock his attacker unconscious.

It was his only chance, because there was no way he would have time to get into his knapsack and draw the Cobra crossbow.

But it wasn't likely. In fact, it was damn near impossible. The man stood in the shadows of the alley about forty yards away. A long throw. And the moment he stood, the man would chop him down with the revolver.

Still, he had no choice. Hawker wasn't about to die on his belly. On the street. At the hand of some goon with fried eggs for brains.

When Hawker leaped to his feet, a number of things happened almost simultaneously.

Hawker took the Randall by the blade and cocked back his arm. The knife was heavy and cold—nearly a pound of handmade stainless and carbon steel fighting knife.

The goon in the alley, realizing this was his chance at a kill shot, steadied his revolver in both hands and brought the front ramp sights to bear on Hawker's chest.

From somewhere behind Hawker, three deafening shots rang out—the line of fire so close that Hawker felt the vacuum impact of the slugs passing his ear.

The goon in the alley was knocked backward as if jerked by

a hawser line, and the revolver tumbled high into the air as the man collapsed, dead.

It all transpired so quickly that Hawker didn't know what exactly in the hell had happened.

He swung around, still holding the Randall.

A square, heavyset figure stepped out from behind the unmarked squad car newly parked at the curb. The streetlight caught his face.

"*Callis!*" Hawker whispered beneath his breath.

Detective Lieutenant Scott Callis holstered his .357 as he approached. He stopped an arm's length away. He looked at Hawker with dark eyes of disbelief, then looked at what had once been the headquarters of the most notorious gang of drug addicts and killers in New York.

The roof of the building had been blown almost completely off. The upper walls had collapsed. The windows blinked with the bright-orange flicker of a spreading fire.

Callis gave a soft whistle and looked back at Hawker. "Jesus Christ," he said in a low voice. "You really did it, didn't you?"

"Thanks," Hawker said, his composure regained. "You saved my life, Callis. I won't forget it."

The cop didn't seem to hear. He seemed in awe of the destruction before him.

"How many were there? How many did you kill?"

Hawker used a weary hand to wipe the blood from the cuts on his face.

The salt on his hand made his face sting.

"I don't know," he said. "I lost track."

Callis whistled again. "Flaherty was right. You're not a man. You're a machine. A fucking killing machine."

Hawker started to say something, but Callis interrupted. "Don't worry, Hawk. These guys weren't up for any good citizenship awards, believe me. And tonight you probably saved three lives for every one you took."

"You think it will soften Blake Fister's operation any?" Hawker asked, studying the ruins of the headquarters.

"I don't know. I doubt it. There's a lot of Blake Fister to go around." Callis slapped Hawker on the shoulder. There was a new urgency in his voice. "Look, you've got to get out of here. That explosion was reported about five minutes ago—I heard the call go out over the radio."

"Yeah? How did you get here so fast?"

Callis smiled. "I tried to get you at your apartment all evening. Finally I decided this might be your night for the big hit. But you've got to get moving. Now. We can write this mess off as a gang war—as long as you're not around to take the blame."

Wearily Hawker adjusted the canvas pack on his shoulder and headed for his van.

He stopped and turned suddenly. "Callis? Why were you trying to get in touch with me tonight?"

The detective suddenly looked uncomfortable. "I was hoping it could wait until morning. You look like you could use some sleep."

"I'm not much for waiting."

Once more, Callis looked at the wreckage. "So I see," he said wryly. "Okay, I'll tell you. It's about that friend of yours."

"Flaherty? The Irish cop out in L.A.?"

"No, the other one. The guy you told me about. Hayes. Jacob Hayes."

Hawker suddenly remembered the sense of dread he had felt only a few minutes before—the strange anxiety about Hayes. "Yeah? What about Jake?"

"It came in over the I.C.I.C. wire late this afternoon. From Grand Cayman. He's been missing for the last couple of days. They found blood in his house down there and there are signs of a struggle. They think he's been kidnapped—or worse."

Hawker nodded, his face showing no expression. "Thanks, Callis. For everything." He turned and began to walk toward his van.

"Hawk. What are you going to do?"

"I'm going to check with the airlines tonight, and if there's no plane out, I'm going to get a few hours sleep. I'll be on Grand Cayman tomorrow."

"If there's anything I can do—"

"I know, Lieutenant," said James Hawker. "And I appreciate it."

NINETEEN

The assassin arrived outside Hawker's apartment just after one.

Lights were on inside the apartment, but Hawker's van was not parked at the curb.

He was not yet home.

But the woman who lived downstairs was.

Renard stood in the shadows of the tenement across the street, watching.

She was up unusually late. Renard wondered if there was a reason. Perhaps she had a visitor. A man staying the night, perhaps.

The assassin hoped not.

He stood outside the brownstone house for a long time, waiting.

So this is what it is all about, he thought, considering the chain of dark German homes. The corporation wanted to buy all of this property, but the corporation's methods had caused James Hawker and his friends to interfere.

Soon they would realize that they had stumbled onto something much, much bigger. And far more dangerous—if they hadn't realized it already.

Not that Renard cared. He cared nothing for his employers or for their business goals.

He cared only for the deed. His craft. His art.

The drama of killing.

This kill, especially.

Hawker and his friends had come all too close to eliminating him on Little Cayman Island. Even now, remembering the agonizing pain he had suffered that night caused a slow cold fury to build in him.

Renard would now make James Hawker pay. But Hawker's death would be no crime of passion. No. That was unprofessional.

Renard had planned his murder completely and carefully. Even the best in his business would admire the masterly touches.

More important, he had forced himself to wait for the perfect moment. It had to be at a time when he and Hawker were alone. He wanted to see the suffering on Hawker's face. He wanted to hear his pleas for mercy.

A clean shot with a revolver was no longer good enough. Indeed, twice already Renard had had opportunities to shoot Hawker.

But he had passed them by. He had passed them by because this was now more than a contract killing. James Hawker had become an obsession. And Renard was going to make his death last just as long as he could.

As Renard thought about it he felt the warm, precoition stir of stomach and abdomen.

It was a pleasurable fantasy, and Renard used it to pass the time.

Finally the woman crossed the scrim of windows into the living room. She pulled the shades, and the living-room lights went out. The hallway light came on, and then what Renard assumed was the bathroom light.

Soon all the lights went out.

Renard snuffed out the cigarette he was smoking and pushed the remains into his pocket.

He waited a full fifteen minutes before walking across the street to the brownstone.

It was 2:48 A.M.

He stopped at the stairs and listened carefully. It wouldn't do for the woman to see him. But no sound came from inside her flat.

Sure that all was well, Renard continued up the stairs. The stairs were old and creaky, so he took them slowly. His one fear was that Hawker would return before he got into the apartment and had a chance to hide himself away.

Three quarters up the stairs, increasingly confident he would make it to the apartment undiscovered, Renard began to take the steps more quickly—and that's when his foot snagged on the piano wire Hawker had planted there.

The assassin stumbled forward and landed hard on the edge of the steps. Then he slid belly-first down the stairs.

Lights flashed on below, and a beautiful blond woman peered out.

"Mr. Hawker?" she asked, squinting into the darkness. "Is that you?"

Still lying on his stomach, Renard tried to match his voice to Hawker's. "Yeah," he said in a soft, husky imitation of Hawker. "Sorry about all the racket. Guess I had a few too many tonight."

"And after that speech you made about being a light drinker," the woman said sarcastically. "Are you all right?"

“Fine, fine,” answered Renard, purposely keeping his back to the woman. “I’ll be okay.”

“Well, you’re probably in no condition to remember, but I’m going to tell you anyway. You have an important message from some corporation in Chicago. Hayes Corporation? Yes, that’s it. They couldn’t get you, so they contacted me through the realtor. You’re supposed to call them immediately. No matter what time it is.”

“Chicago? Right away,” said the assassin. “I’ll call them right now.”

The woman hesitated, a strange expression on her face. She stepped back to close her door, but then looked out again. “Are you sure you’re not hurt, Mr. Hawker? You sound awfully strange. I think perhaps I should have a look at you.”

Brigitte Mildemar pulled her nightgown tightly around her neck, switched on the outside porch light—then froze.

“You’re not . . . you’re not James Hawker,” she whispered. “My God . . . you’re . . .”

Renard stood and faced the woman. There was a light smile on his face. As he began to walk toward the woman, he said, “I brought a present for your friend Mr. Hawker. Such a nice little present. But not nearly so nice as the present I have for you, beautiful lady.”

The woman’s face showed surprise and then shock as the assassin stopped at the bottom of the stairs and pushed back his glasses.

Then Brigitte Mildemar’s lovely mouth contorted into the harsh, taut lines of a terrified scream. . . .

TWENTY

Hawker pulled up outside the old brownstone house on Rhine-strauss at three minutes before three in the morning.

He was surprised to see the lights in Brigitte Mildemar's apartment still on.

It troubled him. He had met the woman only briefly, but the impression she gave was strong and sure. There was nothing about her that suggested the insomniac neurotic.

Hawker switched on the van's interior lights and loaded the Browning automatic's spent clip with fresh 9mm cartridges.

He locked the van and walked to the stairs, holding the pistol in his right hand.

Brigitte's shades were drawn, and the door was shut.

Hawker wondered why the porch light was on. Was she waiting up for him for some reason?

Hawker hesitated, then tapped on the door. There was no immediate response, so he knocked louder.

He listened intently at the window and heard nothing.

Maybe she was out. Yes, that would explain the lights. She was probably out on a date.

Hawker holstered the Browning and walked up the stairs. He unlocked his door and went inside. He put the tea kettle on to boil and opened a bottle of beer to drink while the water heated. Wearily he slipped out of the shoulder holster and laid the weapon on the lamp table beside his bed before calling the airlines.

The first flight to Miami was at 9:15 A.M.

Almost relieved that he would be forced to get a few hours sleep, Hawker began to prepare for bed. But something was troubling him. Hawker couldn't quite put his finger on what.

Did it have something to do with the sudden, overwhelming thoughts about Jake Hayes he had had during the firefight with the Mafia goons? he wondered. He knew Hayes to be a pragmatic and hard-nosed scientist and businessman. But he was also aware that Hayes had traveled the high and private roads of the mind, the ancient roads of *kensho* and *satori*. Hayes had never talked about it. But Hawker had read enough to know that telepathic powers were widely associated with people who had studied the eastern philosophies—though Hawker himself was a cynic about such things.

Perhaps *that* was what was troubling him. Hawker reasoned. Maybe Hayes had been trying to tell him of his own abduction. Unbelievable as it seemed, maybe Hayes was trying to get a message through to him.

On an impulse. Hawker found his address book and dialed the hotel where Hendricks was staying in London.

A bored desk clerk, sounding as if he were stationed on Mars, said Sir Halton had just checked out.

Frustrated, Hawker slammed down the phone.

Hawker grabbed his beer and gulped down half the bottle at one pull. Out in the little kitchen, the tea kettle was beginning to make its first tentative whistling noises. Hawker carried the beer with him while he made his tea. An herb tea. Emperor's Choice. There was something in the face of the man on the tea box that reminded him of Hayes. Some glint of wry wisdom.

Hawker finished the beer, added a glob of honey to the steaming tea, then carried it into the bathroom.

He put down the lid of the stool and sat to take off his shoes. He took off one shoe, then the other—and that's when it hit him. It was the association between shoes and steps.

The wire he had drawn across the steps to his apartment: It was gone. Someone had tripped over it hard enough to knock it down. Maybe that's why Brigitte's lights were still on. Maybe she had come up to leave a message for him, tripped over the wire, and fallen over the railing.

Swearing at his own diabolical cleverness, Hawker ran outside. He leaned over the railing, squinting into the darkness below.

Nothing. No body.

Hawker found the step he had wired. The wire had been snapped clean away.

What in the hell had happened? Had she fallen, hurt herself, and crawled back into her apartment?

Or maybe she wasn't the one who had fallen. . . .

Without hesitation, Hawker drew the Randall knife he still wore on his calf and bolted down the steps.

He tried to look into Brigitte Mildemar's apartment through a crack in the shades.

Nothing.

Hawker banged on the door.

No answer.

He tried the handle. Locked.

Forsaking any thoughts of how foolish he would feel if Brigitte was out on a date, Hawker stepped back and slammed against the door with his shoulder. The door didn't open, but the impact shattered the window glass. Hawker reached through and unlocked it from inside, then swung the door open.

He stood in the doorway, knife drawn.

The apartment was a neater, tidier replica of Hawker's. The door opened into the little kitchen. She had placed a vase of flowers on the kitchen table. The vase had been knocked over, shattered. Flowers were strewn about the tile floor.

Yellow flowers.

The table had been shoved against the refrigerator, and two chairs were overturned.

A torn blouse lay in a heap on the floor with the flowers.

A white blouse.

The same blouse she had worn, buttoned so primly, that same afternoon.

There was a smear of blood on the blouse.

"Brigitte!" Hawker called hoarsely. *"Brigitte!"*

No answer.

Hawker moved smoothly through the kitchen, the Attack-Survival knife vectoring ahead of him. He found the wall switch, and the living-room lights flashed on.

A whimpering sound brought his head swinging toward the hallway which led to the bedroom.

A woman stood in the hallway, looking pale and shrunken in the bad light. Someone's fingernails had dug three blood-red trenches down her cheek. She wobbled back and forth, as if about to faint. Finally she reached up and grabbed the doorsill to steady herself.

"My God," Hawker whispered. "What are you doing here?"

"I was outside," the woman said in a weak and shaken voice. "I heard a scream. I thought I might help. I found my way in here. Then someone . . . someone attacked me. A man. A man with a gun. He is gone now. Oh, I am so glad he is gone."

Hawker hesitated, then sheathed the Randall knife. He hurried to the woman's side and took her arm to give support. "Are you all right? I'd better call an ambulance—"

"No!" the woman interrupted. "Please. I'll be fine. I just need to rest. To recover. Something to drink."

"But Brigitte—where is she? Is she—"

"Please," the woman cut in. "I must sit down. I must. Before any more questions, *ja?*"

Without another word, Hawker led the old blind German woman to the couch and turned his back to go to the kitchen.

TWENTY-ONE

Hawker found a bottle of white wine in the refrigerator and poured two water tumblers half full. As he closed the refrigerator door, he looked in to make sure the old woman was okay.

She sat on the couch with her knees pressed together. She wore the same baggy dress she had worn on the day he had first met her. Despite the struggle, she still had the white cane. She propped it against the couch as she brushed back her gray hair and fumbled in her little purse before producing a tissue.

She dabbed at the blood on her face and sat staring straight ahead. The black glasses she wore gave her face a skeletal look.

Hawker walked into the living room and stopped a body length away from her. He held out the wine, but she made no effort to take it. "What were you doing out so late?" he asked, as he took her hand and placed one of the tumblers in it.

Her head swiveled toward him as she sipped the wine. "Time means nothing to me. Is it late? *Ja, es ist* late. But you were kind to me, so I made something nice for you. A nice man, you are, *ja*."

Hawker remained standing. "Do you have any idea of who the guy was who attacked you? How long ago did he leave?"

The old woman felt the lip of the glass with her fingers and guided it back to her lips. "One half of an hour? Fifteen minutes? I do not know."

"And he took Brigitte? Or is she still—"

"The lady with the pretty voice? Oh, it was so terrible! How she screamed! *Ja*, the man, he took her. In a car. A very loud car. Such a noise it made as he pulled away."

Hawker studied the woman's trembling hands as she drank the wine. He was silent for a moment. "You're still upset. Can I get something else for you? A cigarette, maybe?"

Her laughter was a rough cackle. "A cigarette? No. I am an old-fashioned woman. I do not smoke." The black glasses searched above Hawker's head. "A bit more wine, perhaps—but first, this thing I made for you."

She found her old purse and began to feel through it. After a moment, she produced something wrapped in aluminum foil. She unwrapped the foil to reveal a small brown loaf. "A fruitcake." She smiled. "I made it for you, as I said I would." Her smiled broadened. "You are so deserving."

Hawker took the fruitcake. He smelled it. "I hope I can find a way to repay you," he said. He put the cake to his lips and turned away chewing as he returned to the kitchen. He poured another tumbler full of wine and carried it back to the living room.

He could feel the old woman's glasses tracking him.

He stopped in front of her and held out the glass. "The fruitcake is very good," he said. "Would you care for some?"

"No," she said quickly. "My appetite, it is not good. But the wine, I like. You have more wine?"

Hawker held out the glass—and let it slip through his fingers.

When Renard's hands lunged instinctively to catch it, Hawker knocked the black glasses from his face with a crashing overhand right. The blow sent the assassin tumbling sideways off the couch.

The Frenchman got shakily to his knees. Blood rivered from the gaping split on his cheek, and the gray wig had turned almost backward on his head. He would have appeared strangely comical if it wasn't for the venomous look on his face.

"It's too late, James Hawker," the assassin hissed. "You're a dead man. The cake—you ate it before you found me out! And it has four times the saxitoxin you gave me. One bite! One bite and you are gone!" His laughter was shrill. "Now you're going to find out what it's like to die from poisoning—just as I almost did back on that godforsaken island. Now you're going to find out what happens to do-gooders who poke their noses into Fister Corporation's business."

"What did you do with her, Renard?" Hawker whispered hoarsely. "Where's Brigitte Mildemar?"

"It's not going to matter, where you're going, Hawker!" the assassin half shouted. "The pain—it's going to start soon. You're going to feel like someone has built a fire in your brain. Then the fire is going to drain down into your stomach, and every muscle in your body is going to wrench—"

Hawker took a half step and kicked the Frenchman's mouth closed with his bare foot. "The woman, Renard—where is she?"

The assassin pulled himself off the floor and wiped the blood from his face. His eyes studied Hawker closely, looking for the first signs of the slow and agonizing death he had planned so carefully. They were dark eyes, with a wild, bright gleam: the eyes of a madman.

Hawker's cold blue eyes didn't flinch. Slowly he held out his right hand and opened his fist. The cake was there—uneaten. A cruel smile touched Hawker's lips. "Your fingers, Renard. I suspected it was you anyway, but your fingers gave you away. The nicotine stains didn't match up with an old German woman who claims not to smoke." Hawker's smile broadened slightly. "And now I'm going to get the chance to repay the favor."

The assassin moved with startling quickness. As Hawker stepped toward him, Renard rolled to the side and came up with the white cane. He swung it with whistling velocity, and Hawker ducked just enough to catch the brunt of the impact on his shoulder. Even so, it knocked him down.

Again the Frenchman swung at him, and Hawker rolled away as the cane cracked against the floor beside his head. Hawker got his right foot up and wedged his heel into the assassin's groin. Renard grunted with pain, doubling over. Hawker got to his feet, slapped the Frenchman's face twice with his open hand, then grabbed him by the throat and ran him backward against the wall. He used pressure on the killer's throat to force his head up. "You don't look well, Renard," Hawker whispered, his lips pressed near the assassin's ear. "Maybe you need a little something to eat. Are you hungry, Renard?"

As Hawker brought his hand up, the Frenchman tried to force the cake away from his lips. "No," he begged. "Kill me, if you have to. But not like this. Please. . . ."

"Where's the woman, *asshole?*"

"The . . . bedroom . . . tied up," Renard sputtered, still trying to fight Hawker's hand away.

"Did you hurt her?"

"She tried to fight me," he said, pleading. "You must understand. It is my job—"

With cold indifference, Hawker punched upward with his left knee. When the Frenchman's mouth opened involuntarily to scream with pain, Hawker shoved half the poisoned cake into his mouth, then gave him a measured slap in the throat.

"Bon appétit," Hawker snapped.

The assassin gulped and then his eyes grew wide with terror. "Oh, my God," he whispered. "No . . . no . . . *no!*"

Hawker was unprepared for what happened next. The Frenchman gave an animallike scream and then dove for the purse he had carried in his disguise as an old woman. He brought the stub-nosed revolver out so quickly that Hawker had time only to dive blindly for cover.

The shot was oddly muffled.

Hawker looked up to see the assassin sprawled backward on the couch. A momentary fountain of blood gushed from his head, then settled into a steady black seepage.

The Frenchman's eyes were glassy and wide. His right hand trembled—clenched white on the grip of the revolver. For a microsecond, he seemed frozen in the transition between life and death. Then the muscles contracted, and his hand flapped hard against the floor as the last rigidness of life melted away.

The assassin had taken the ultimate contract—his own.

This time, there was no doubt about it. Renard was dead.

Hawker turned away, feeling, for the first time, the searing pain in his left shoulder where he had been hit by the cane. He rubbed the welt momentarily, then hurried down the hall, flipping on lights as he went.

Brigitte Mildemar was in the bedroom.

The terror was plain on her face when Hawker first stepped into view, but then she visibly relaxed when she saw that it was not Renard.

The Frenchman had stripped the clothes off her, and she lay on her back, naked. Her legs were hobbled at the ankles, and her arms were tied behind her.

In another situation, she would have been quite beautiful: dusky-brown pubic hair arching upward as she struggled against the ropes; hips curving into long, feminine legs; the soft pink of nipples jutting upward on her small, firm breasts.

But here, bound and gagged, she looked pathetically small and vulnerable. In one motion, Hawker yanked a blanket off the dresser and spread it over her, then drew out his Randall knife. The seven-inch blade razored through the gag, then he gently rolled her over on her stomach and cut away the ropes.

She made small whimpering sounds as she tried to pull her arms away from the small of her back. Realizing that the nerves in her arms had gone numb, Hawker rolled her onto her back and began to massage her hands.

"Oh, my God," she cried, "I was so afraid it would be him again. I couldn't have stood that."

"Are you hurt, Brigitte? I'm going to call a doctor. It can't do any harm to—"

"No," she said quickly. "No, he didn't . . . he just hit me and tied me. But he didn't have time to. . . ." Her blue eyes couldn't quite meet Hawker's. "You came then. Before he could." Without looking at him, her hand squeezed Hawker's hand gently. "Thank you," she said. "I really don't think I could have stood it."

"You may not thank me after you've seen what happened. The man who attacked you—he's dead."

For just a moment, her voice regained a small bit of its fire. "I'm *glad,*" she said. "Oh, Mr. Hawker, I was so frightened. I heard you come in. I could hear you two talking. I wanted to scream out, to warn you. He looked and sounded so much like an old woman, I didn't think you could possibly find him out. And the way you kept demanding to see me. . . ." For the first time, her eyes looked into Hawker's. "I can never ever repay you for that. Never."

"Brigitte," Hawker pressed, "I can understand your being reluctant about seeing a doctor. It'll be painful to talk about this with anyone else. But there was blood on your blouse. I saw it. In the kitchen."

She trembled slightly and pulled the blanket tighter around her neck. "It was his blood. I tried to scratch his eyes out. That's when . . . that's when. . . ." Her voice faltered as a sob wracked her body. She held her arms out, childlike, and Hawker pulled the woman close to him, holding her, stroking her hair as she wept.

"He's gone now," Hawker kept repeating. "You're safe."

"Why did he attack me?" she cried as the words and the terror drained out of her. "It was like something out of a horrible nightmare. My God, it was so awful. Why? Why would he do such an terrible thing to me?"

Still sobbing, she looked at Hawker as if he might hold some answer. "I've got to tell you the truth, Brigitte," he said softly. "The man's name was Renard. He was a very bad man. A killer. He has killed a great many people. But he would never have attacked you if he hadn't been looking for me. I brought this on you. It is my fault. I had no right to place you in danger, and if I had used my brain for just a moment, I would have realized that was exactly what I was doing by moving in here."

"He wanted to kill you?" she asked in a small voice.

"Yes. He wanted to kill me."

Slowly she drew away from Hawker. She released the blanket and wiped her eyes with her hands. The blanket fell away, showing the small, firm breasts. She made no effort to pull the blanket back. "He called you a 'do-gooder,'" she said. "He said you had poked your nose into Fister Corporation's business. Do you work for the government, Mr. Hawker?"

"No." He smiled. "And the name is 'James.' Sometimes I do people favors. That's why I came here—to do a favor. But, unfortunately, what happened tonight makes it necessary for me to leave even sooner than I had planned. You're going to have to call the police, Brigitte. And you're going to have to tell them exactly what happened. Compromise yourself in no way, because if you lie to them, they're going to find out."

"But, James," she insisted, "you didn't do anything wrong. You probably saved my life—"

"Maybe," Hawker cut in. "But that won't make any difference to them or to the legal system. I would still be detained. And I can't afford that."

"You're a criminal?" she asked softly. "You're wanted?"

Again Hawker smiled. "No. But a friend of mine is in trouble. Serious trouble. I have to go to him."

The woman settled back on the bed, studying his face carefully. She brushed a lock of blond hair from her forehead, then reached out and traced Hawker's square jaw with her index finger. There was nothing flirtatious about it. It was more as if she were trying to see him more clearly by using the sense of touch.

"I felt very bad about the way I talked to you this evening," she said finally. "Normally I wouldn't have. But there is something in your eyes . . . something beneath the coldness there. You seem to have a goodness in you."

"There are a lot of people around who would give you a pretty convincing argument about that."

She shook her head, as if refusing to even comment on it again. "When are you leaving?" she asked.

"Now. As long as it takes to get my gear together."

"Please," she whispered. "Please, not yet." Again, her eyes refused to meet Hawker's. "I would like . . . like to be held. Just held. For a while. It's been so long since I've been close to anyone, it would make me feel so much better." She turned and looked into Hawker's face. "Please, James. Please?"

Hawker sighed, trying not to look as uneasy as he felt. He had no time to play nursemaid, and no desire to act as the woman's therapist. Only politeness kept him from looking at his watch. "For just a little bit, Brigitte," he said finally. "Then I have to go. Really."

She lifted the covers in silent agreement, and Hawker slipped beneath them, holding the woman's warm nakedness in his arms. She snuggled in close to him, whimpering softly. Hawker stroked her hair for a time, then felt himself drifting off into the gauzy world of sleep, exhausted.

He awoke suddenly in darkness, surprised to find his body aroused by something. The woman had turned off the overhead light. A lamp on the vanity bathed the room in a soft yellow glow. She was trembling terribly, as if with fever. Hawker would have thought her ill, were it not for the way her small hands were stroking him. He wondered how she had gotten his pants undone without waking him.

Noticing that he was awake, her hands bolted away from him. "I'm sorry," she said, breathing heavily. "I had no right—"

Hawker cupped his hand behind her head and pulled her face to his, kissing her gently. "It's okay," he whispered. "It feels nice."

Her voice shook, as if she were about to cry again. "It's just that . . . that it's been so long since I've been with a man. I dreamed that we were . . . that we were making love. Maybe it was a way of erasing something so terrible with . . . with something good. I guess I started doing this in my sleep. You felt so strong that I didn't stop when I woke up."

Hawker guided her hands back to him, then touched her hard nipples with his lips. "Neither of us is asleep now," he said softly, then he kissed her again, harder, feeling her hips rise against his hand; groin soft and wet and wanting.

For the first time, she smiled as a giant shudder passed through her body. "I'm glad," she whispered. "I'm glad you're awake. Now I can show you what I was dreaming. And, James?"

Hawker had kissed his way down her firm stomach, and now

his lips had found the soft pubic thatch. She smelled warm and sweet. "Yes?" he said.

"James. I've thought about it. While you were sleeping, I thought about it. And I don't want to be here to face the police either. James—I don't know where you're going . . . but I want to go, too." As Hawker lifted his head to speak, she pressed her index finger against his lips. "Not now," she whispered. "Please, not now. Later, James." As Hawker returned to what he had been doing, the woman moaned softly. "Much, much later. . . ."

TWENTY-TWO

Loughros Moor, Ireland

Hendricks nodded at the guard, then walked into the dun-colored mass of Gweebarra Maximum Security Prison.

The prison was a bleak fortress squat on a bluff above the gray sweep of the Atlantic. It was four stories high. Outside, the main wall was fenced by ten-foot-high chain-link and rolls of concertina wire. Between the main wall and each fence was a ten-meter killing area.

From the cells on the fourth floor of the penitentiary, inmates could see the craggy hills and the endless moor that rolled along the edge of the Atlantic, away from the prison.

Reggie Collins was on the fourth floor. He was in a ten-by-twelve cell with a shielded overhead light bulb, a metal cot, and an aluminum commode.

It had not been easy for Hendricks to arrange to see him. It had meant telephoning three of the most honored names in Great Britain and calling in some old and personal debts.

But he had done it. Now he had what he wanted: a personal interview with his old comrade, just the two of them, away from the prying electronic listening devices of the prison's visitors' room.

Hendricks followed the custodian through the maze of bars and electric gates to the cage that held the man who had been found guilty of treason and was rumored to be Hendricks's nemesis of old, the Druid.

Collins stood at the window of his little cell, staring out over the Atlantic. The custodian rattled his keys and turned the lock. "Collins—you've got a visitor," he said in a bored monotone.

Reggie Collins turned slowly. His gaunt eyes seemed to have difficulty adjusting to the dimmer light. "Who . . . who is it?" he asked in a submissive, uncertain voice.

So shocked was he by the man's appearance that Hendricks couldn't answer for a moment. During the war, Collins had been the embodiment of all that was good and brave in Her Majesty's forces: tall, articulate, handsome. Now he was drawn and shriveled. His black hair had turned white, and his ruddy skin, gray. There was a palpable air of decay about the old British agent with whom Hendricks had once worked so closely.

"It's me, Reggie," he said finally. "It's me, Halt Hendricks."

"Hank?" the man asked, taking a step closer as the guard locked the door behind Hendricks. "My Lord, can it really be?" Collins's face slowly contorted into a mixed expression of pain and wild joy as he reached out and took Hendricks's hand and wrung it with emotion. "You don't know how I've dreamed of this moment, Halt. You have no idea! Through this whole bloody affair, during those endless interrogation sessions, throughout the trial—even *here*—I kept asking to see you. And now, by Godfrey, you're here!"

Collins's face was locked in a brave smile, but then the smile gradually collapsed into an anguished look as he began to cry. His whole body shuddered, and Hendricks did not back away as Collins leaned against him, bawling like a child.

Hendricks patted his shoulder tenderly. "It's okay, Reg," he said. "Steel yourself, man. I had no idea what you were going through. They never tried to get in touch with me, or I would have come."

Collins turned away in an effort to gain control of himself. Finally he rubbed his eyes and motioned for Hendricks to take a seat on the little cot. "I'm okay now, Hank. Bit embarrassing, that." He sniffed and cleared his throat as he sat on the floor, his back against the concrete wall. "This has been such a bloody, rotten business. Thought it was quite the joke when the buggers came after me as a traitor." He forced a laugh that couldn't hide his bitterness. "Called me the bloody *Druid!* Can you imagine? *Me?*" He looked anxiously at Hendricks. "But you can tell them the truth, Hank. Only you know the real truth. You know I was never a blasted Russian agent. You know that it was only a deep cover—"

"What happened to the records at MI-5, Reggie?" Hendricks interrupted. "Certainly they should have dug them out and presented them to the Assizes, considering the severity of the charges against you."

Collins shook his head nervously. "No records, Hank."

"But there *were* records, for God's sake—"

The old agent smacked a withered fist against his hand. "I know! But they were lost or stolen—probably the latter. At any rate, there were no records to be found." A pitiable laugh slipped from his lips. "Rather funny, really. I was so careful to build a convincing cover in those days that it was my own cleverness which sent me here. Most of the evidence used against me was evidence I had planted during the war." Collins cocked his head unexpectedly, as if listening to some distant sound.

"What is it, Reg? Do you hear something?"

Collins's eyes were abruptly clouded by a foggy, faraway look. "It's the bloody screaming, Halt," he whispered after a moment. "The screaming. I can stand the cold water and the bad food and the roaches, but it tears at my insides when I hear those poor buggers being tortured."

Hendricks listened carefully.

A cold thrill moved through him.

There were no screams.

There was only the hushed silence of the sea crashing onto the bluff outside.

Collins, quite obviously, had been pushed over the brink of his own endurance, pushed toward the dark chasm of insanity.

"Reggie," Hendricks said gently. "I want you to listen to me. I'm going to get you out of here. You're going to be all right. But first, I need to know some things—things you know more about than anyone on earth."

"Of course, Hank," Collins said distantly, still preoccupied with the terrors of his own mind. "What do you want to know?"

Hendricks took off his derby and hunched closer to the shrunken man. "I want you to tell me about Martin Bormann, the man who was supposed to carry Hitler's legacy on to future generations. I remember your insisting after the war that Bormann was not dead."

Reggie Collins's eyes seemed to clear momentarily. "Quite right," he said. He rubbed thoughtfully at his ears before adding, "It's more than just speculation on my part. Bormann and his young aide had exacting plans—plans made, actually, by Hitler himself—to escape by plane. They were to leave Rechlin Airbase. The plane they were to use was a specially built Junker Three-ninety, which carried thirty thousand liters of fuel and had a cruising range of eighteen thousand kilometers. It could have taken them, quite easily, to Paraguay."

"Or Nicaragua?"

"Of course."

"What makes you think they got the chance to use it, Reggie?"

"It's rather simple, Halton. When the Russians finally got to Rechlin, the Junker was gone. Someone used it. And, as you know, neither the bodies of Bormann nor his aide have been found. It was not because the bodies were not sought, either. Bormann was such a sadistic little animal, the Russians had quite a thing about finding him. But I rather think Bormann's aide was even worse. A nasty bit of work, he was. A young rough named Fisterbaur."

Hendricks shivered slightly. "*Fister*baur?"

"Yes. Bormann recruited him from the interrogation staff at Auschwitz."

Now more than ever, Hendricks felt the urge to answer the unconscious summons that had called him to help his friend and employer, Jacob Hayes. He felt as if he should race immediately from Gweebarra Prison to Belfast and catch the first direct flight to Miami. If he hurried, he could possibly be landing in Grand Cayman in less than fourteen hours—only nine hours, counting the time difference. Instead, he took a deep breath and forced himself to remain calm. He said, "There's one more thing I would like to discuss, Reggie."

Collins's head tilted again, as his own private terrors threatened once more to take control. But then he shook himself, forcing his attention on Hendricks. "Anything, Hank." His smile was touchingly vulnerable. "We have no secrets from each other."

"Yes, Reggie, that is true. And it must stay that way. Apparently, there was speculation that you were the Druid—the one Abwehr agent we were never able to find. Only two living people—you and I—could know for certain that you are *not* the Druid—"

"Wrong," Collins cut in. "There are three people who know. *He* knows, Hank. The Druid knows. I have had plenty of time to think about why I was chosen as a scapegoat. And make no mistake about it, a scapegoat is exactly what I am. The reasons always point directly back to the man who, for so long, has been a question mark in both of our careers. Of course, any finger I might point now would be dismissed as the desperate ravings of a convicted traitor." The man's gaunt eyes looked deep into Hendricks's eyes. "He knew I was a potential danger to him, and he found his way to destroy me, Halton. You should be forewarned that any interest in my case will make it necessary for him to destroy you."

Hendricks's jaw tightened and his voice was cold. "He hasn't destroyed either one of us, Reg. Not yet." He pulled out his pocket watch and checked it perfunctorily. "We have fifteen minutes left, Reggie, old horse and in those fifteen minutes you're going to tell me everything you know, everything you suspect about the Druid of modern days—and that includes keying me on some of the Druid ciphers you unraveled. And then, if that lovely jailer of yours is a little late, we'll get rooting on a plan to nail that bastard. Because we *are* going to nail him, Reg. The two of us will have a nice cup of tea on the son of a bitch's grave. That I promise you."

Reggie Collins's eyes misted as he smiled for the first time in a very long while. "Thank you, Halton," he said softly, fighting back the tears. "Thank you so much for giving me hope. . . ."

TWENTY-THREE

Grand Cayman

On the long commercial flights from New York to Miami, from Miami to Owen Roberts Airport on Grand Cayman, James Hawker wrestled with the uneasy feeling that he was too late.

When the beautiful Brigitte Mildemar's voracious sexual wanting was finally satisfied, then and only then did she remember that "some corporation in Chicago" had left a very important message for Hawker.

Hawker had immediately thrown back the covers and walked naked past the cooling corpse of the assassin to the phone.

The message was important all right. It was also confirmation that the strange foreboding Hawker had experienced was chillingly accurate.

One of Hayes's trusted secretaries enlarged on the details provided by Callis: Jacob was, indeed, missing and feared kidnapped—or worse. Traces of blood had been found in the bathroom of his island cottage. The blood matched Hayes's type. The Grand Cayman police force was investigating but had found nothing yet. Hayes's last communication to corporate headquarters consisted of a manila envelope.

At Hawker's insistence, the secretary read the contents to him. While the material could have been better understood by a business expert, Hawker deciphered enough to know that the reports contained serious and incriminating information on Fister Corporation.

After instructing the secretary to make copies of the financial data and lock the copies away in a variety of places for safekeeping, Hawker hung up and returned to the bedroom.

Brigitte had pulled a white T-shirt on that was not quite long enough to cover the smooth swell of hips and the burnished glow of pubic triangle. Her short blond hair was mussed with their lovemaking.

She was packing a suitcase, humming nervously.

Calmly Hawker walked over and began to unpack her bag.

"What . . . what are you doing?" she had stammered.

"You're not going," he said easily.

"But you promised. And after what we did—"

"I didn't promise. And what we did was fine for both of us. But sex has nothing to do with business—something too many women conveniently refuse to understand."

Brigitte stepped away and thrust her fists on her hips. "You're going to leave me here with that . . . that . . . *body?*"

The outrage in her voice was so ripe with indignation that Hawker had to fight back a smile. "If I don't the police will be after you for suspicion of murder. If you stay, they'll just be after me."

"And that's supposed to make me feel better?" she demanded.

"It's not supposed to make you feel better or feel worse. That's the way it is. Period."

For a moment, Hawker thought she was going to try to bury one of her small fists in his face. Instead, she gave a sputtering cough of frustration, then plopped down on the bed.

"It's not ladylike to pout," he said with a smile.

"I'm not pouting!" she yelled back. She sniffed and tugged the T-shirt down over her thighs. "I'll never forgive you for this—I swear it."

"I don't remember asking for forgiveness," said Hawker as he pulled on his clothes. He notched his belt tight, then leaned over and gave her a quick kiss on the cheek—and ducked as she took an open-handed swing at him. Hawker wagged his index finger at her. "Temper, temper, dear." He leaned down, kissed her again (on the mouth, this time), ducked another wild roundhouse, and headed out the hall door. "I'll see you when I get back, Brigitte, darling."

"I'll see you in hell first!" she yelled after him.

"Better that than another night in The Bronx," Hawker said over his shoulder, leaving.

At Owen Roberts Airport, Hawker didn't even bother to dicker over the price of a rental car. He selected the most dependable-looking vehicle available—a dented and well-traveled Mustang—and paid in cash.

Because of the inevitable layover in Atlanta, his only choice was the late flight into Grand Cayman. So, by the time he got his duffel bag and leased the car, it was well after midnight.

It was a balmy, warm night with moon. An oily breeze blew

over the reef, across the island, carrying with it the Caribbean smells of citrus, diesel fuel, sea wrack, and jasmine.

Hawker drove north on Crewe Road, north toward Bodden Town and Jacob Hayes's cottage.

Traffic was sparse as he sped along past late-night juke joints and the dimly lighted island homes with their clotheslines and sand yards and conch-shell borders.

At South Bay, he turned right and bounced down the private drive until it ended where the Caribbean Sea spread away toward Nicaragua, vast and silver-laced in moonlight.

Palm trees bowed over Hayes's cottage, rustling in the sea breeze. Ghost crabs the size of rats clattered away as Hawker got out, threw his duffel bag over his shoulder, and headed for the front door.

Immediately, he stopped.

There was a light on inside. A dim light, flickering in the living-room window.

Hawker unzipped his duffel bag and took out the only weapon he dared check through commercial customs: the Randall Attack-Survival knife.

He drew the knife and peeked through the front window.

The light was made by a single candle.

A man sat cross-legged on the floor beside the candle, staring at the wall. His hands were folded in his lap, and his eyes were unblinking, as if in a trance.

The man should have been wearing a loincloth. Instead, he wore very proper gray worsted slacks, dress shirt, and vest. His jacket had been folded over the chair.

It was Hendricks.

Hawker put the knife away, tapped on the door, and then stepped inside. Hendricks got quickly to his feet and switched on one of the table lamps.

"Christ," said Hawker, "you look like you haven't slept in a week."

"Nice to see you, too, James," Hendricks said dryly. "You've heard about Jacob?"

"Yeah. A cop friend of mine in New York told me, then I called corporate headquarters. Jake had dug up a lot of dirt on Fister. I guess they figured he was getting too close." Hawker put his duffel bag on the floor and went to the kitchen to find that Hendricks had already boiled water for tea. "How long have you been here, Hank?"

"About two hours. Just long enough to stop at Western Union, check with the local authorities, and come here."

"Western Union? Why Western Union?"

"Had to send a telegram to an old friend of mine named Druid," answered Hendricks as he put bags of Indian green tea into the two mugs.

Hawker looked at him carefully. Hendricks seemed oddly distracted, as if subdued by worry. "We're going to find Jake," Hawker said softly. "I promise you."

"Are we?" said Hendricks. "The police say they have absolutely nothing to go on. And I have the very unhappy feeling that, if we don't find him tonight, Jacob won't live to see another day." The butler sipped at his tea and walked to the candle he had lighted. He touched his fingers to his lips, and the flame hissed as he extinguished it. Hendricks began to say something, faltered, then pressed on. "James?"

"Yeah, Hank?"

"James, very early yesterday morning, I was awakened from a sound sleep by thoughts of Jacob. Strange thoughts. They were almost . . ."

"Overpowering?" Hawker inserted.

"Yes," Hendricks said quickly. "It was almost as if—"

"As if he were trying to communicate with you?" Hawker cut in again.

"Exactly," Hendricks agreed, giving Hawker an odd look. "How did you know?"

"What time was it you woke up?"

"A little before seven A.M., I would imagine."

"What time would that be in New York?"

"Oh . . . just before two."

Hawker nodded emphatically. "I had the same kind of thoughts at the very same time," he said. "I couldn't shake them—and, believe me, in the situation I was in, it should have been easy." Hawker motioned toward the candle. "Is that what you were doing when I came? Trying to get back in touch?"

"It's called *zazen,*" Hendricks said. "Sitting meditation. Jacob gave me a little instruction, but it always struck me as rather silly. Still," the butler added thoughtfully, "it seemed as if I was getting some very strong impressions just before you came. Very cold impressions. Bleak. Hellish." Hendricks looked quickly at Hawker. "That's why I said I didn't think Jacob could hold out another night—if he's not already dead."

"Do you think you could find him?" Hawker asked. "Were the impressions that strong?"

Hendricks shook his head and snorted in frustration. "Think

of what you're saying, James. Do you really think we have a chance of finding a man hidden away on this island through the use of this . . . nonsense?"

"Mumbo jumbo," corrected Hawker.

"It's absolute rubbish," agreed Hendricks.

A slow smile formed on Hawker's lips. "The only weapon I have is a knife."

Hendricks thought for a moment. "I flew the Trislander down. The taxi driver who brought me here was quite upset by the weight of one of the bags."

"Weapons?" Hawker asked.

"I think Thompson submachine guns qualify as weapons." Hendricks sniffed.

Hawker clapped him on the back. "Let's load up and hit the trail, O Swami."

TWENTY-FOUR

For more than an hour they drove aimlessly through the dusky moonlight, scouring the island's back roads.

There were certain craggy areas of bluff and sea that drew Hendricks's attention: Half Moon Bay, Gun Bay Village, Ireland Bluff. All seemed to capture the bleak mood of the impressions that had come to him through meditation.

But they found nothing. The dark houses taunted the two men. Hayes could have been hidden away in any of them.

Hawker drove while Hendricks navigated—the two of them feeling increasingly desperate.

Hawker skidded left, then sped south at Old Man Bay, jamming the Mustang through the gears. On Crewe Road, he headed back through the modern city of Georgetown, then north along the hotels of Seven Mile Beach. Intent on their strange mission, the two men said little. Hendricks spoke only to give directions; directions that came, it seemed to him, on empty whim.

Finally, in frustration, he banged the dashboard with his fist and exclaimed, "Damn it all, James, this is absurd! Jacob *may* have been communicating with us, but the power came from *him*. He's the one who's had the training in . . . in this mystic business. Not me. I'm beginning to feel like a perfect fool."

Hawker slowed and pulled over to the side of the road. The island was sparsely populated there, the houses set back deep behind fences and heavy foliage. He put the car in neutral and locked the brake. "You may be right, Hank." He sighed. "The only impression I've gotten in the last half hour is that I'm going to burst if I don't pee."

He opened the door, stepped out, and began urinating into the ditch. "Hank," he said suddenly, with a growing excitement in his voice. "Describe the place again, the place you think they might be holding Jake."

"No certain place," Hendricks answered wearily. "It was just a bleak feeling. Rugged. A lot of rocks—"

"Not that. Earlier, you described it as 'hellish.'"

"Well, yes, but—"

Hawker poked his head back in the car. "Hank," he said anxiously, "we're there! We're in Hell."

"James, dear boy, I have no idea what you're talking about."

"The road sign," Hawker insisted, "it says 'Hell.' We're in the village of Hell." Hawker slid back into the car and started the engine. "Damn, why didn't I think of it to begin with? I noticed it on the map the last time we were here. The sea, the craggy rocks, the bleakness—this place has it all."

"Even so, I wouldn't get my hopes up—"

"But I do have my hopes up, Hank. Damn it, we're going to find him. We've *got* to find him."

Driving slowly, but not so slowly as to arouse suspicion,

they cruised past a series of large estates that were built on bluffs overlooking the vast Caribbean. One in particular caught Hawker's attention: It was a massive stone house, three stories tall, surrounded by mature tropical trees and a high iron fence. Spires of igneous rock, gray in the moonlight, jutted above the crash of sea fifty feet below the house.

Lights twinkled through the trees.

"People are still awake there, Hank," Hawker said anxiously. "What do you think?"

"Yes," Hendricks whispered almost to himself. "*Yes*. It could be. . . ."

"We don't have time for 'could be,' Hank," Hawker pressed. "This is either the place where they have Jake locked up, or it isn't."

"But, damn it all, there's no way I can know for sure—"

"Yeah, there is," Hawker insisted. "We're going in to take a look. Then we'll know."

Hawker drove up the road another hundred yards and pulled off into a gumbo limbo thicket. The two men got out quietly and slid the thirty-round detachable box clips into the old Thompson M1A1's.

"Christ," whispered Hawker, "I feel like a movie gangster, carrying one of these things."

"Very popular with those of us who lived through the war," Hendricks said. "And rather appropriate, considering who we're going after."

Hawker looked at him. "Is that supposed to mean something?"

Hendricks favored him with a wry look. "Let's just say we've gotten into something bigger than any of us ever dreamed possible. There's not time to explain now."

"Hank," said Hawker, "I hate it when you're cryptic."

"Tut-tut, dear boy. The explanation can wait. Jacob can't."

The two men made their way down the road, then cut into the shadows. At the iron fence, Hawker helped the older Englishman over the top, then climbed over himself.

It was one twenty A.M.

The estate consisted of a several-acre rectangle of well-kept trees and scrubs: coconut palms, gumbos, mango, and Australian pine. The mansion sat at the back of the lot, overlooking the sea.

They discovered that the fence had been wired for silent intruder alarm when they were only a few hundred yards from the house.

And it was not a pleasant discovery.

TWENTY-FIVE

As they moved past a jasmine copse, two figures suddenly sprang out at them.

Hendricks was knocked violently to the ground, while Hawker managed to keep his feet. He used the heavy butt of the Thompson to crack down on the neck of the man who had jumped him, then swung it like a saber at the man who now stood over Hendricks.

The butt of the submachine gun caught the attacker high on the right shoulder, spinning him around. Hawker saw the automatic in the man's hand lift to fire. He dove low and hard, his shoulder aimed at the man's knees. There was a deafening *kerwack* that, at first, Hawker thought was the automatic.

It wasn't.

The man gave a hideous scream and fell to the ground, clutching the kneecaps that had been crushed backward by the impact of the collision. Hawker drew the Randall from its calf scabbard and drove the seven-inch blade deep between his ribs. The man shuddered, then went still.

Hawker wiped the knife clean in the sand, then got shakily to his feet.

"How's the other guy?" he whispered.

Hendricks dropped the lifeless wrist. "Dead. That crack on the back of the head did it."

"Parapsychology aside, I would guess this is the place."

Hendricks picked up his weapon and observed dryly, "You have a wonderful talent for saying the obvious, James."

"Jeeze," retorted Hawker. "I save your life, and you're *still* snotty."

"Not at all, dear boy. Much thanks." He began to walk toward the house. "Now let's go save Jacob's life."

There were about twenty yards of open lawn between the house and the wood. They knelt at the edge of the foliage, peering out. Two more guards stood at the door: men in gray uniforms, holding machine pistols. Hawker could tell by the way their heads vectored back and forth that they were wondering what had happened to the other two guards.

"Any ideas?" Hendricks whispered.

"Yeah. We could blow them away from here with the Thompsons—but they'll probably kill Jake or try to sneak him out the moment they realize they're under attack."

"Exactly."

Hawker wiped the sweat off his chin and flung it at the ground. "So I want you to start moaning—"

"What?"

"You heard me, Hank. Moan, damn it. Like you're hurt. And make it convincing."

As the Englishman began dutifully to groan, Hawker slipped off into the shadows.

When the guards heard the noise, they hesitated, then came in single file, their automatic weapons moving back and forth. Hawker waited until they were both among the trees before he jumped them—hitting them both at once and knocking them to the ground. He jammed the survival knife through the spinal column of the first guard, then swung around in one motion and clubbed the second guard flush in the face with his right fist. But, as the guard stiffened from the blow, his finger contracted on the trigger of his machine pistol, releasing a deafening spray of bullets.

"Shit!" hissed Hawker.

Immediately more lights began to flash on in the house. "We've got to charge them," called Hawker as he sprinted off toward the front door. "Just keep my tail covered, Hank!"

As Hawker reached the steps, the door swung open to reveal another man wearing the same gray uniform. Hawker lifted the Thompson and squeezed off three fast shots. The slow .45 slugs splattered the man's chest open, like a five iron through a tomato. Hawker hurdled the corpse and dove through the open door.

A half-dozen more guards in various states of undress were running down a massive winding stairway.

A gigantic red, white, and black swastika flag was draped from the domed ceiling.

As Hawker sprayed the guards with fire, they tumbled backward, spilling over the railing. One of the men grabbed the flag in his death throes, pulling it down with him.

The pale tile floor began to pool with red.

Behind him, Hawker heard more automatic fire. A moment

later Hendricks stepped through the door. He surveyed the corpses coldly and said, "There are three more outside."

Hawker made no comment. He went from body to body, until he finally found a man who was not quite dead. Hawker grabbed his hair and yanked his head up so that he was eye-to-barrel with the Thompson. "Where is he?" Hawker snapped hoarsely. "Where's Jake Hayes?"

"He's . . . he's above. The top floor . . ."

Hawker and Hendricks didn't wait to ask any more questions. They ran up the marble stairway, two steps at a time. Hawker was well in the lead when he reached the third level of the house—so the lone guard standing there brought his weapon to bear on him.

The marble railing shattered beside him as Hawker lunged belly-first into the hall, skidding on the slick floor. Hawker twisted as he skidded, and the Thompson belched out a pattern of .45 slugs that ripped through the guard's chest.

The guard screamed bearishly and fell dead.

Hendricks arrived a moment later. "That was the door he was guarding?" he asked, nodding toward a double door mid-way down the hall.

Hawker got quickly to his feet. "Yeah. Let's go."

When they were both ready, Hawker nodded and they swung open both doors at once—then froze at what they saw.

The room was large, done in white marble, like a shrine. One whole wall was covered by another gigantic swastika. On either side of the flag were large oil portraits. One, plainly, was Adolf Hitler. Hawker didn't recognize the other—but Hendricks did. It was Martin Bormann.

But the Nazi paraphernalia was not what arrested their attention.

In the middle of the room, Jacob Montgomery Hayes was strapped naked to a stainless-steel table. A man in a white smock stood over him—an older man, in his mid-sixties. His greased black hair protruded from the white surgical cap. He had a pinched, meaty face, a mole above his left cheek, and searing blue eyes. The scalpel in his hand was pressed against Hayes's neck.

"Unless you drop your weapons immediately," the man said calmly, "I will kill him."

Hawker looked at Hendricks incredulously. "Who in the hell *are* these guys?"

Hendricks did not answer. "If you kill our friend, Herr Fisterbaur," Hendricks snapped, "I will take great personal pleasure in seeing that both you and your superior, Martin Bormann, die very slow and painful deaths."

"Bormann?" echoed Hawker in disbelief. "As in the Third Reich—"

"So," interrupted Fisterbaur, "you know something of us?" He smiled, still holding the surgical knife to the neck of the unconscious Hayes. "Unfortunately, your threat carries little weight as far as Chancellor Bormann is concerned. He died eleven years ago in Nicaragua. Of natural causes, I might add—though I doubt that is of any interest to you."

"And that's when Hitler's fortune was passed on to you?"

Fisterbaur's smile broadened. "Not just the Fuehrer's fortune. The Fuehrer's *legacy*. And, in my American role of financier Blake Fister, I have handled that stewardship quite well, I think. The fortune has tripled—but that is nothing compared to the great strides I have made in politics. In El Salvador, Argentina, France—yes, even in America and the Fatherland, people are rising up again to shoulder the great cause."

"Until now," cut in Hendricks. "Your secret is out, thanks to that man on the table—a far better man than you and the other animals who 'shoulder' your cause, I might add."

The stainless-steel scalpel flashed in Fisterbaur's gloved hands. "I will not argue the point," he said, bristling. "We will not be stopped here. We have come too far, worked too hard." He paused, then added, "You English pride yourselves on holding steadfast to the gentlemanly code. We of the Reich also embrace that code. Now, as an officer and a gentleman, I promise that if you drop your weapons, your lives, and the life of your friend, will be spared. All I ask in return is the safe delivery of the financial records on Fister Corporation that you have stolen."

When the two men did not react immediately, Fisterbaur pressed the knife against Hayes's neck. A thin red line of blood appeared. "I promise you," Fisterbaur hissed, "that I would gladly give my life to take his—now, drop your weapons!"

"We have your word as a gentleman?" Hendricks asked, his face a cold mask.

"Yes!"

Hendricks held out his submachine gun and dropped it heavily on the floor. "You have our word as well," he said without emotion.

"Right," said Hawker without conviction. He looked at Hendricks, looked at the gun on the floor, then held out his Thompson as if to drop it—but didn't. Instead, he mashed the trigger down on automatic fire, pouring a steady stream of .45 slugs into Fisterbaur's chest.

The surprise impact knocked the scalpel high into the air as the German backpedaled across the room, his velocity surging as each new slug cut through his body. His back crashed into the window behind him, and he exploded through the glass, screaming a high, agonized wail as he fell the fifty feet to the wave-cleansed rocks of Hell.

In the fresh silence, Hawker punched out the spent clip of the Thompson.

The cheap metal clattered on the floor.

He looked at Hendricks and shrugged. "I'm no gentleman," he said.

Hayes stirred slightly on the table. His face was corpse-white, and his body logged the horrors he had suffered during his captivity. He was covered with cuts and bone-deep bruises.

Hendricks checked his pulse while Hawker sprinted to the phone and called an ambulance. He returned carrying a sheet.

As he covered Hayes, he whispered in his friend's ear, "You're going to be okay, Jake. We're going to get you out of here."

Hayes's face twitched and his eyelids fluttered open. He focused on Hendricks, then Hawker. "I've been to a wonderful place," he whispered. "A wonderful land . . ." Then with a shudder, he lapsed once again into unconsciousness.

Hawker looked anxiously at the Englishman. "I think we both ought to ride to the hospital with him. He doesn't look good, Hank. I think we should both be there."

The grief was plain on Hendricks's face. Even so, he shook his head. "No," he said. "You go. I have to stay."

"But why, for God's sake?" Hawker demanded. "Damn it, we've killed them all. I don't understand what in the hell was going on yet, but I do know that Fister Corporation no longer exists."

"Sometime soon I have an appointment with an old friend," Hendricks explained simply. "It's an appointment long overdue."

In the distance, there was the anxious wail of sirens. Hawker tugged the sheet snugly around Jacob Montgomery Hayes who, near death, seemed bathed in the soft, cool light of peace.

"Hank," Hawker said again, "I hate it when you're cryptic."

EPILOGUE

The Druid's limousine went down the winding drive toward Fisterbaur's mansion at 9 A.M.

Hendricks sat on the steps, feeling older and wearier than he had ever felt in his life.

In his right hand he held a freshly loaded German Luger, model PO8, he had found while going through the stacks of books, diaries, and microfilm that were Adolf Hitler's legacy to the future.

When he saw the dark Cadillac, with its tinted windows, coming down the lane, he slid a shell into the breech, covered the automatic with his derby, stood, and checked his pocket watch.

The last bodywagon had pulled out only two hours before; the last policeman, only forty-five minutes ago.

Hendricks had not slept in nearly thirty hours.

The Englishman waited calmly while the car drew slowly to a halt in front of the house and the door on the driver's side swung open. He was not surprised to see who got out.

"Good morning, Laggy," he said as Sir Blair Laggan of London stepped from the car. "Or rather should I say, 'Good morning, Herr Druid'?"

Sir Blair was dressed in a light-blue sea-worsted three-piece suit that was still rumpled from his all-night flight. His heavy face was flushed, and his expression seemed a mixture of confusion and anxiety.

"Druid?" He sputtered. "For God's sake, Halton, what are you talking about? My secretary told me your message said to come immediately, that it was a matter of life and death—"

"Your *secretary?*" Hendricks whispered as the sudden confusion he felt slowly dawned into the shock of realization. "How could she have possibly—"

"How could I have read a message that only the Druid could have decoded?" asked a woman's voice from the inside of the limousine. The long, perfect legs of Mary Kay Mooney speared out the door as she slid across the seat and stood behind Sir Blair, straightening her skirt. She wore a white blouse and a rust-color jacket that matched her auburn hair perfectly.

In the soft tropical light, her beauty would have been dazzling—were it not for the lethal-looking Browning Hi-Power automatic she held.

Blair Laggan looked at the gun incredulously. "My God, Mary Kay, what do you think you're *doing?* You have absolutely no reason to carry—"

She swung the gun toward Sir Blair's head and, without warning, fired. Laggan's head burst into a fountain of red as he was slammed to the ground, his last words unspoken.

Then she swung the gun back toward Hendricks. The

expression on her face was cold and unemotional. "Actually, Sir Halton, I'm quite impressed by you. I thought Chancellor Fisterbaur would certainly kill you and your associates." She looked at the drying bloodstains on the steps of the mansion meaningfully. "Obviously I was wrong."

"Your *father*," whispered Hendricks. "Your father, Sir Blair's orderly—*he* was the Druid. All those years, and he was right under our very noses."

"Yes." She smiled. "And, during all those years, he told me what fools you were. What fools, with your nauseating honor and your hypocritical standards, using brave Irish lads to fight the Germans while starving their families through your brutal system of peonage. That's why he made a pact with the Third Reich and became the Druid. And that's why I took up the cause after his death. Working at Sir Blair's data center was no accident, you see. It offered double benefits: I had access to the world's computers, and I could keep a close watch on you old fogies from MI-5 as well. Laggy did so like to stay informed about his old mates."

She chuckled, but the gun did not waver. "When a telegram arrived addressed to Sir Blair—a telegram supposedly written in code by Herr Fisterbaur—I knew, of course, it was really from you. We had done away with that code long ago." Her smile broadened. "But it was the perfect opportunity for me to eliminate the only two remaining men on this earth who even knew about the Druid."

"You forget about Reggie Collins," Hendricks stalled. "You may have fixed the records well enough to have him convicted of treason, but Reggie is far from dead."

"Yes, but he *is* going quite completely insane. Anything he may have to say about the Druid will be dismissed as the ravings of a lunatic." She motioned with the Browning. "Enough talk," she said. "You are holding a weapon behind your derby. I want you to drop it. Now."

"That would be rather silly," Hendricks said calmly, "since I clearly intend to use it to kill you."

An amused expression crossed the woman's face. "Come now. One of the Queen's knights shooting a woman? I know you English too well."

Hendricks thought for a moment. He had never felt so weary. Maybe it *was* his time to go. Laggan, whom he had wrongly accused of being the Druid, was dead. Collins was locked away in slow ruin. And his beloved friend, Jacob Hayes, was dying—if not already dead. Perhaps his era *had* come to an end: the era of fighting for just causes; the era of good men who lived by codes of honor; the era when right and wrong were two clearly defined things, and people respected the responsibilities of both.

Sir Halton Collier Hendricks gave a long, tired sigh and let the derby fall to the ground, exposing the Luger he had hoped to use to kill this great ghost from the past.

He smiled. "You know," he said, "this is the second time this morning I have been imposed upon by being a gentleman." He nodded to himself. "And, sadly enough, Miss Mary Kay Mooney, I'm afraid you are right. I really can't bring myself to shoot a woman—even a woman as misdirected as you."

"But I can," said a cold voice from the edge of the trees.

Both Hendricks and the woman turned to see James Hawker standing beneath the burnished limbs of a gumbo limbo, the Thompson submachine gun braced firmly against his shoulder.

He began to walk toward them, with the barrel of the Thompson fixed on the lovely body of the woman. "Now drop the gun, lady," he said softly. "Drop it, or I'll give you your first and last lesson on American men."

The woman made a motion as if to toss the Browning Hi-Power away, then snapped it toward Hawker, jerking off four quick shots.

Hawker dropped to his belly, and the old submachine gun rattled its death chant as the Druid's white blouse exploded into a pattern of scarlet holes. She crashed backward into the open car, her skirt flying up over her hips.

She twitched once, then lay still as Hendricks rushed to her side. He straightened the skirt down over her panties, then touched her perfect face. The woman's eyes quivered wide with shock and pain. Her lips moved as if to speak, and Hendricks bent close to hear. With a final agonizing effort, her lips pursed—and then she spat squarely into Hendricks's face.

"Sieg Heil!" she hissed.

Her face went slack as she fell back on the seat, dead.

Hawker took the Englishman's shoulder and turned him away. "I'm sorry," he said. "She gave me no choice."

"I know," Hendricks said softly. "She was going to kill me." He wiped his face wearily and looked at Hawker. "How's Jacob doing? What did the doctors say?"

Hawker studied the corpse of the dead woman for a moment, then turned away, sickened by the utter waste of it. "He's been through a hell of a lot these last few days," he said finally. "The doctors could only guess at some of the things they did to him, but it must have been one long nightmare. They said most men would have died after the first few hours."

"But how *is* he?" Hendricks insisted, trying to keep the emotion out of his voice.

Hawker's eyes came to rest on the turquoise edge of sea and sky where frigate birds wheeled high over a school of bait, soaring on hot-air thermals, and for some reason they brought back Hayes's words:

"*I have been to a wonderful place . . . a wonderful land. . . .*"

Hawker cleared his throat. "They say he's dying, Hank." He turned and squeezed the old butler's shoulder. "But who's to say? Doctors have been wrong before. And the two of us know that stranger things have happened. . . ."

ABOUT THE AUTHOR

Randy Wayne White was born in Ashland, Ohio, in 1950. Best known for his series featuring retired NSA agent Doc Ford, he has published over twenty crime fiction and nonfiction adventure books. White began writing while working as a fishing guide in Florida, where most of his books are set. His earlier writings include the Hawker series, which he published under the pen name Carl Ramm. White has received several awards for his fiction, and his novels have been featured on the *New York Times* bestseller list. He was a monthly columnist for *Outside* magazine and has contributed to several other publications, as well as lectured throughout the United States and travelled extensively. White currently lives on Pine Island in South Florida, and remains an active member of the community through his involvement with local civic affairs as well as the restaurant Doc Ford's Sanibel Rum Bar and Grill.

OPEN ROAD
INTEGRATED MEDIA

CPSIA information can be obtained at www.ICGtesting.com
Printed in the USA
BVOW08s1450240816

460046BV00001B/13/P